The Blood of Maria

Lydia Harbinger

Published by Lydia Harbinger, 2024.

This is a work of fiction. Similarities to real people, places, or events are entirely coincidental.

THE BLOOD OF MARIA

First edition. December 11, 2024.

Copyright © 2024 Lydia Harbinger.

ISBN: 979-8230539995

Written by Lydia Harbinger.

Author's Note

This novella contains very dark subjects which may be triggering, and a full list of warnings is available on the author's website.

Reader discretion is advised.

Chapter One

Maria wandered across the lobby, each step graceful yet always on the verge of tripping. Her hand was wrapped around a drink, her third or fourth based on the gentle sway serpentining through her body.

Henry watched transfixed as her lithe form approached the reception desk. She leaned against the wooden surface, a drop of condensation trickling down her forearm and pooling against the desk, where her elbow was crushed bloodless.

Henry pretended to straighten a stack of papers Jenny had left on one of the shelves, though they had already been arranged with Jenny's characteristic fastidiousness. Henry did not always grasp her organizational structure at a glance, as it was so rarely alphabetical. Yet, when it was understood, there was a beauty to it that he found himself envying.

Henry flicked through the papers, almost recreationally searching for the pattern, but he would steal a glance at Maria in those moments when he sensed he was unobserved. The top two buttons of her dress had come undone, and there was an anemic blush spreading across her ample bosom. The faint, drained, pinkish flush would have gone undetected, were it not for the training Henry's eye had undergone over the year he had already spent in the hotel's employ.

Henry reckoned he knew every freckle and every line which graced the woman's body. Her heavy drinking made her unaware of his lustful study, or at least this is what Henry told himself when his gaze stretched minutes beyond what was safe.

Jenny returned to the lobby, carrying a cocktail napkin, which she set on the desk next to Maria. She could never meet Maria's eye during moments of the older woman's intoxication, and Jenny skirted the desk and slipped into the backroom, disappearing just as quickly as she had arrived.

Henry had once wondered why Alan seemed so unfazed by his wife's far too public drinking in his hotel, but these days Henry felt a little surer of the reason. Alan seemed to regard his wife as decoration, no more conscious than the bronze statue of Minerva which stood silent and proud at the opposite end of the lobby.

It seemed an apt comparison to Henry. Beneath the polished, heartbreakingly beautiful façade lurked an immeasurable depth of wisdom and cunning. Behind Maria's stilled tongue lay a mind she'd silenced for the sake of the trinkets around her. Every afternoon she began the laborious process of drugging herself into submission, becoming nothing more than mildly interesting décor.

She leaned forward, and the fabric of her dress fell slightly more open, offering a coveted view of her round breasts. Henry could feel his blood rising, and his breathing becoming strained. He left his idle study of the papers in front of him, to instead grip the edge of the reception desk. His mind flooded, by this point involuntarily, with images of what he would do if given half the chance. He would use his body to make her feel loved, to show her every ounce of the devotion she had inspired in him from the moment of their first meeting.

He had long since given his imagination free rein, picturing again and again every hidden curve of her body, imagining what her long, raven-black hair would look like wrapped three times around his fist. He had spent long nights visualizing himself buried deep within her, the hardness of his cock a tribute to her ethereal beauty. He would shed his blood, sweat, and tears to prove to her that she was worthy of such devotion.

Perhaps Henry was a masochist.

His attentions would never be returned.

Just as Maria's husband regarded her as ornamentation, the decoration he felt he deserved, Maria saw Henry as a utility. Necessary, but unworthy of thought beyond whether or not it operates as expected.

He could hardly blame Maria for this. Nearly every woman he had met treated him the same, even women far less captivating.

Henry was not unattractive, at least this is what he saw in the mirror: his skin was unflawed; his hair was light brown, ample, and kept neatly brushed back; his body was well-formed and athletic; and he dressed as well as his income would allow. Yet, there was something about him which provoked an instinctive rejection by the fairer sex. It was nothing dramatic, but he knew he had never been seen as a sexual being at all. Women neither confided in him, nor sought his attentions. Instead, he existed within a sexless, passionless void.

He thought he had grown used to it, but every so often, something would remind him of his buried aspirations, and he would feel the crushing defeat with an undeniable freshness.

Though faced by such indifference, Henry had experienced a call to action only the day before, when Jenny's eyes had lingered just a little too long on the man at the hotel bar, while they habitually passed over Henry. It was then that he had hatched the plan which would find traction within the hour.

WHEN JENNY RETURNED to the desk and began searching for something within the shelves, Henry watched from the corner of his eye as she visibly stilled.

"Did a guest leave this here?" she asked, holding out the book.

Henry began to walk to her side, but Maria was faster, curiosity giving her steps a momentum and steadiness to which Henry was unaccustomed.

Maria took the book from Jenny's hands and surveyed the cover, her eyes widening in surprise.

Henry did not have to look. He knew what was depicted on the cover perfectly well, though it was the soft, worn spine which he had been touching throughout the day. It had almost acted as a talisman, something which steadied him, promising a new, better tomorrow.

He felt a flush rise through him, a kind of transmuted aggression as he viewed the scene: Maria holding the pornographic material in her beautiful hands, her lip hitching slightly as she viewed the naked, immodestly splayed blonde on the cover.

Then, when the moment had nearly dissolved, he spoke up.

"It's mine," he said.

Both women turned. Their surprise was evident, but Henry could not tell whether their shock was due to his confession, or whether they had never heard him speak so forcefully, so confidently in their presence.

Maria gripped the book a little tighter, before shifting it, so that the explicit image was pressed to her outer thigh. Without a word or backward glance, she stepped past the reception desk and into the backroom where her husband was working.

Jenny kept her eyes averted, returning to sorting papers she had already organized. She would not look at him, but Henry could see the heat in her cheeks.

A moment later, Alan stepped out of his office, and motioned for Henry to follow him. There was a sudden pain in Henry's throat, and he wondered if adrenaline could ulcerate flesh. There was nothing left for Henry to do but accept whatever fate lay behind the door.

Alan seated himself behind the desk, and motioned for Henry to take the chair opposite. Alan slapped the book down on the desk, so that the woman photographed was facing Henry.

Alan was a man of medium height, with a broad frame. His hair was blonde, but just beginning to grow white at the temples. He wore his wedding ring and a fraternity ring, alongside a well-polished silver watch. His sleeves were permanently rolled up to the elbows, and his tie was never knotted less than five inches from his throat.

"So, my wife tells me that this is your book," Alan said.

"It is," Henry said.

"And why?" Alan asked, before clarifying. "Why was it found behind the reception desk?"

Henry paused, but he was already well-practiced in the lie he would tell.

"I forgot I had it on me, so I tried to hide it before a guest could see. I am very sorry that the women came across it before I could find a better place," he said.

Alan shook his head. "You're staying in one of the rooms on the second floor. Why not excuse yourself and leave the book in your private quarters?"

Henry shrugged. "I suppose I should have. I just didn't think of it."

Alan smiled, before picking the book up, glancing at the cover, and idly thumbing the contents.

"I don't think you're that careless, not by a long shot. If I had to guess, I'd say you set the stage perfectly for this book to be found," he said.

The breath hitched in Henry's throat as he contemplated never seeing the inside of this hotel again, of leaving behind the woman who had come to haunt his thoughts with her mere unattainability.

His face must have visibly blanched, because Alan set the book down, a strange grin stretching across his face.

"Don't worry. I'm not going to fire you," he said lightly. "In fact, I have something that I think you'll find very interesting. How about we take this conversation to the bar across the street?"

Henry couldn't imagine what Alan had in mind, but the leer shaping on his employer's face made his blood run cold. If the man just wanted someone to watch stag films with, Henry was sure there was someone who would make a better companion than his employee: a man over twenty years his junior.

Still, Henry could hardly say no.

Chapter Two

They walked through the hotel lobby, Alan with his coat draped over his arm. Henry knew that the book had been slipped into one of the pockets, and he followed meekly behind.

Jenny was manning the desk, and her eyes followed the pair. Henry knew she must have assumed that Alan was walking Henry out, perhaps to break the news of his firing. Henry almost wished he could tell her that he had no expectation of termination, but there was still an uncertainty in his heart. He could not imagine what waited for him in the bar across the street.

There was a dusting of snow on the sidewalk when they stepped out. The sun had set about three hours earlier, and the true cold of the night was only just beginning. Alan kept his coat over his arm, and Henry tucked his fingers into fists as he felt the early bite of the air. His breath clouded before him, and he watched the small puffs beneath the golden streetlamp lights, as they crossed the street.

The warmth of the bar was almost saccharine, and Henry loosened his tie to avoid sweating too profusely. The bar's congregation had thinned to the typical late night, weekday crowd, so he and Alan were able to find seats at the far end of the bar where no one would overhear their conversation.

Alan ordered a double whiskey, while Henry asked for a stout. Within seconds of the spirit being poured, Alan emptied the glass in a single, fluid motion, and signaled for the bartender to pour him another.

"I'm not sure I understand why I'm here," Henry said, when he felt Alan was waiting for him to speak.

Alan smiled. "What if I told you that I had a secret, and it's something that you'll find to be of interest. But, if I tell you my secret, you'll have to keep it too."

Henry shrugged, growing more nervous by the minute. He didn't like the way Alan was looking at him, and he felt that the book's cover should have given the man some idea of where his interests lay.

"Let me ask you a question," Alan said, continuing. "Do you think my wife is a beautiful woman?"

Henry only nodded, afraid that if he opened his mouth, he would begin to tell Alan that Maria had occupied every one of his fantasies from the moment he had laid eyes on her. He would tell Alan that Maria possessed a beauty and poise that he could not relate to, but desired to somehow destroy.

Alan chuckled lightly to himself, before emptying his fresh glass. The bartender poured a third without prompting, and Henry wondered just how familiar the bartender was with the other man's drinking habits.

"So, back to my proposition," Alan continued, eyeing the drink without reaching out to touch it, not yet. "It may surprise you to know that there is more to my little hotel than meets the eye. I can't tell you how shocked I was when I found out that there is a blind hallway connecting every floor in the building."

Henry truly could not anticipate the man, so he waited in perfect silence.

"I think you might get a thrill out of seeing a little more of my wife," Alan said with a conspiratorial smile. "You know what I mean: what she's like during those more intimate moments. I can offer you a window to a view you would never see otherwise."

"I'm not sure I understand," Henry said, half-believing the entire thing was some kind of joke, or maybe a trap.

Alan wrapped his fingers around the glass, before smiling at Henry again. This time, there was an impatient edge to the crooked grin.

"You understand perfectly, so don't try to play games with me. This is an opportunity that will not come again, so you decide what it means to you. You'll keep your job either way, so don't worry about that."

Frankly, the job was now the last thing on Henry's mind.

"So, you're asking if I would like to secretly watch your wife from a hidden hallway?" Henry asked.

Alan shrugged. "Is that so bad a prospect? If you could see what I bring out of that woman when we're alone together..."

Henry stared down at the barroom floor as he contemplated what accepting this offer would mean. He would be given unprecedented access to the hidden life of the woman he had come to love from a distance. He would see her at her most unguarded, see her when she was not drunkenly wandering the public spaces of the hotel. He would see what she was like when she was not under the appreciative gaze of every man present.

Yet, it would also mean seeing her with Alan. Henry tried to imagine what that would look like. He tried to summon up an image of Alan heaving on top of her, degrading her body in ways Henry could not quite bring himself to picture. It was a steep price to pay, but one that Henry could hardly refuse.

"So, you would like for me to see you...with her," Henry began, believing that Alan could hardly blame him for wanting to banish any uncertainty from the deal.

Alan watched Henry, entirely at ease.

"Yes, Henry, I would like for you to watch me have sex with my wife. It's something I've always wanted, but the opportunity never really presented itself. I'll be honest and say that when I saw that book, it just cemented an idea I've had practically since the day I hired you," Alan said. "Now, I have a theory about why you left the book there, but I'd like to hear your thinking."

For the first time in the conversation, Henry became embarrassed. He could feel his cheeks heating with shame, but hoped it was not too visible in the low lighting of the bar. In truth, he could only think about how foolish he had been. Given the distance of only an hour, the ploy seemed childish at best, a pathetic cry for attention.

"I just wanted one of them to notice me," he said.

Alan nodded. "You think the women ignore you, seeing you as a friend or coworker at best, but never understanding that you are a man, with red-blooded drives."

Henry nodded.

"And you thought that by displaying your desires blatantly, you would get that attention," Alan continued.

Again, Henry could do nothing but nod.

"Well, I am happy to say that you've caught my attention," Alan said, letting out a bark of a laugh. "I'm sure I'm not exactly the person you'd fantasized about, but I hope what I'm offering isn't too poor a consolation."

Henry was quiet, before finally breaking his own silence. "So, how does this work?"

Alan pulled the inciting book from the pocket of his coat, and laid it down on the bar. He opened the back cover, and flattened the pages under his palm. He asked the bartender to give him a pen.

"So, you're in room 211, right?" Alan asked, once he had a pen in hand.

"Yes," Henry answered.

"Alright, so do you remember how I told you we had no choice but to put you into a connecting room, but that the room next to yours was used for storage?" Alan asked, continuing before he could get a response. "Well, that wasn't entirely true. In fact, I put you in that room because the adjoining door opens into the hidden hallway. Like I said, I've had big plans for you from the beginning."

Alan began to sketch a rough map on the inside of the back cover. "If you turn left, you'll come to a set of stairs. You'll take these up three flights, to the fifth floor. There, you'll walk to the very end of the hall. You'll see an empty picture frame hanging on the wall. Take it down, and you'll see an opening, which looks through a one-way mirror into my bedroom. I'll let you know what times to be there."

Alan closed the book, and handed it back to Henry.

"So, how does that sound?" he asked.

Henry stared down at the back cover of the closed book. "It sounds like a dream," he said, though unsure of whether that was a good thing.

Alan laughed again, before raising his glass. Henry met the glass with his own, and the clink seemed strangely dull. Henry realized he had not touched his beer once during the conversation, but now it was all he could do to slow his drinking to a more measured pace. He emptied the glass and ordered another. Alan clapped him on the back, and ordered another himself.

The pair continued drinking for the next hour, and by the time they left, Henry was steadying Alan, acting as a somewhat unstable crutch.

Back in his bedroom, Henry found he had no energy left for the world. He collapsed onto his mattress, not even bothering to untuck the blanket. He passed into a restless, drunken sleep from which he would emerge only further troubled by the night's revelations.

Chapter Three

In the morning, Henry only gradually recalled the conversation with Alan. Beneath the cold light of day, his plan to plant the pornographic book filled him with the shame of one who should, by all reasoning, have known better. The latter half of the night was still unreal to Henry, and Alan's proposal seemed built on tenuous ground.

Henry decided to begin the day as though nothing had happened the night before, and only time would tell if Alan was sincere in his bizarre proclamation.

He took extra care with his appearance, and went downstairs. Half of the day had passed, and Henry was nagged by his empty stomach. He slipped out the side door to grab some lunch before beginning his shift.

He dreaded seeing Jenny.

Jenny had a way of drawing attention to your shortcomings precisely by trying to avoid them. She was overly fastidious, truthful to a fault, and had a kind of small-town innocence which she wore on her sleeve.

Henry often looked at her admiringly, though knowing that there was nothing for him there.

Jenny was, of course, already in place behind the reception desk when Henry returned. She made a point to meet his eye, and to fix a smile on her face.

"How are you doing?" she asked, nervous in her sympathy.

Henry shrugged. "I'm doing alright. Sorry again about that book yesterday. I was hoping to stow it until the end of my shift. I imagine it wasn't exactly something you wanted to see."

Jenny laughed lightly, but with a precision that smacked of control.

"No harm done. I'm just glad we avoided an incident," she said.

Henry wondered what she meant by that.

The day passed in excruciating increments, each measured out by Henry's nervous, halting heartbeats. He had seen Maria only briefly, and she had ignored him completely before settling down at the hotel bar. He would glance at her every hour or so. But she was always facing away.

Alan too had remained far from the lobby, and Henry felt a strange tension in the air. He had been left more or less alone with Jenny, and her company was anything but reassuring.

Finally, it was time for Henry to return to his room. The day was slow as usual, and he often wondered why the small hotel had never even halfway filled.

Henry was just beginning to believe that the conversation with Alan had perhaps been a dream fragment, bleeding over into real life, but then he received a message on his cell phone.

Be there in five minutes

IT WAS ALAN'S NUMBER, and Henry could already feel his heartbeat quicken. He retrieved the book, on which Alan had laid out the map and directions.

Henry tried to open up the door adjoining the next room, but found it was locked. He looked around, and realized that a key had been left on his bedside table. He stuck it in the lock, and it turned easily.

Henry switched on his cell phone's flashlight, and stepped into the space behind the door. He found himself in a small vestibule which opened into a narrow, unfinished hallway. Henry took the first turn shown on the map, and his shoulder brushed both walls with each step, sparking a kind of claustrophobia. He shifted his shoulders to better navigate the space, but the closeness of the walls was ultimately inescapable.

When he reached the stairs, he realized the age of the hallway. He half expected the deteriorating wooden steps to give way under his weight. They creaked fearsomely, but held.

When he reached the fifth floor, he walked down the hallway, shining the light tentatively until he found the empty picture frame Alan had described. He switched off his light, before taking down the frame, setting it silently against the wall.

In front of him lay a wide opening. There was a tinted glass covering the squared aperture and this must have been the one-way mirror. The room on the other side was large, it seemed to be three of the largest suites in the hotel combined into one space.

The bed was made of a dark wood, and had a canopy of a black and gold woven material. This matched the blanket on the bed, and the sheets folded over the top were a muted gold. Every corner of the room was richly furnished, and a Persian rug stretched the impressive length of the room.

Maria was seated in front of a vanity. She was wrapped in a black silk robe, which opened at the front to reveal the lace covering her bosom. Henry could see that she was dressed in a short nightgown, its material matching the robe.

She was still wearing her makeup, and brushed her hair slowly, her eyes seeming to track the gentle movement of the bristles through her long, soft, raven black hair. There was a sorrow to her eyes, which it surprised Henry to see was even present during those moments she thought herself to be alone.

The door opened, and Henry could almost believe he saw the door handle turn before he heard the noise, dampened as it was by the layer of glass.

Alan stepped through the door, and Maria turned lazily to greet him. Her hand on the brush stilled, but only for a moment, before resuming its meditative practice.

Alan strode past Maria to the place where Henry was hidden. Alan checked his appearance in the mirror with a smirk, his conspiratorial gaze directed to a place just inches above Henry's eyes. Alan flattened his blonde hair with his palm, offering one final expression of knowing to Henry, before turning back to the room.

"How has your day been?" Alan asked as he stalked toward where Maria sat, still brushing her hair.

She shrugged, looking at Alan's reflection in the mirror, but never turning to meet her husband's direct gaze.

Alan closed the distance between them, and gently wrested the brush from her grip. Maria's fingers tightened around the air, forming an incomplete fist, before falling limply to her side.

Alan took Maria's elbows, and brought her to stand in front of him, her body still facing the vanity mirror. He drew her into a sort of adversarial embrace, before guiding her to the center of the room, to a place between the one-way mirror and the foot of the bed.

Maria was now facing Henry. He could see an element of annoyance in her eyes, though even this was cooly masked behind her habitual expression of indifference.

Alan's fingertips ran along the silk robe, before guiding it from his wife's shoulders and letting it fall to the floor around her ankles, where it formed a dark, shimmering pool of fabric.

Maria was now dressed only in the short nightgown, detailed with a delicate black lace. Henry could see the swell of her ample breasts beneath the thin material, and his eyes lingered on her bare legs, imagining what was concealed beneath the short hem of the nightgown.

He would not have to wonder long, as this too was slipped from her body, and Maria was left naked, the back of her body pressed against her fully clothed husband.

Henry drank in the sight of her bared breasts, with their ample curves and areolas just a shade darker than her light brown skin. His eyes travelled to the place between her legs, where there lay a triangle of dark hair which was just as lustrous and enchantingly dark as the raven tresses gracing her head.

Alan stepped to her right side, before guiding her to her knees in front of him. She dutifully undid his belt and unzipped his pants, drawing his engorged cock free. Alan's hand found the back of her head, and guided her towards the tip of his large, heavy member. He pressed the tip to her lips, and Henry watched enraptured as Maria's mouth opened to accept her husband's length.

Alan kept his left hand on her head, as she established a rhythm, working her beautiful mouth over every inch of him. It seemed that Alan was intent on giving Henry a good view, angling himself so that every inch of his cock could be seen disappearing into her mouth.

After a few minutes of this, Alan drew Maria up from the ground wordlessly, and brought her to the side of the bed. He laid her down, so that her ass was against the edge of the bed. Without undressing himself, Alan slid his cock between her legs and deep into her sex.

At this, Maria gave a small moan, and Henry felt a thrill run through his body. He reached down, to where his cock was already hard, and unzipped his pants. He gripped his erection tight in his right hand and began to stroke himself as the scene continued to unfold before him.

Alan began thrusting into his wife, causing a shift in the bed with every hard drive forward. Maria's breasts jogged as her body was jostled, and Alan possessively gripped her shoulder, before moving down to knead her breast, the pace of his thrusts increasing.

The sounds of their bodies meeting, and of the bed creaking beneath them bled through the glass, and Henry tried to quiet his own labored breathing as he stroked faster. He pressed his palm against the wall, eagerly watching the way Maria's legs wrapped around Alan's body, accepting every inch of his driving cock deep within her.

Henry watched the hard member being thrust into her again and again, and found he could contain himself no more. His cum spilled onto the wall, and he caught himself in a series of small gasps.

Henry's orgasm was quickly followed by Alan's. He watched as his employer pulled himself free from Maria's body and stroked himself over her stomach.

At this, Henry turned away.

He placed the picture frame back over the hole in the wall, and switched the flashlight on. He made his way back to his bedroom on unsteady feet, his mind a battleground of emotions. He was glad to have seen Maria in her most vulnerable state, and could feel the early resurgence of arousal at the thought of her perfectly formed, naked body.

However, this was intermingled with a kind of hatred and jealousy towards Alan. The other man's display of possession could not have been clearer, and it was likely this which had driven the entire performance. It sat uneasily within Henry's breast, and his helplessness only gave dull teeth to his anger.

He locked the door, and threw himself onto his bed. He knew no sleep would come that night, and resolved to relive every moment of that viewing, creating a pornographic tableau to which he could return again and again, promising many long hours of arousal, shame, and envy.

In his heart, Henry was sorry for Maria, to have her trust so absolutely violated by the man she'd bound herself to. Yet, he knew he would watch her again.

Chapter Four

As Maria walked through the lobby in the late morning, her mind wandered absently to the things that had brought her there. She'd never paid too much attention to psychology; she'd never paid too much attention to anything. She was one of those people who didn't walk through life so much as they floated. She learned early on that the problem with allowing yourself to drift, is that you have little control over where exactly you end up and, in truth, this is how Maria found herself living in this hotel, her days spent between the bar, the reception desk, and the back office. She didn't do much, and it seemed her husband didn't mind.

Then again, there was a time when she hadn't minded much either.

If she had taken more of an interest in herself earlier on, she might have ended up someone else. Then again, a burst of true motivation could also have left her in a world to which she was wholly unsuited.

Trying to silence those ideas which would every so often force themselves through a vacuum of thought, Maria sat down at the hotel bar, and the bartender immediately brought her a gin and tonic, with an extra shot of gin. She smoothed her raven hair back, still a little uncomfortable whenever he handed her usual to her.

"Anything else I can get you?" he asked.

She shrugged.

The guest who had come to haunt the hotel bar in the previous weeks looked her over. She didn't even have to glance in his direction to know that she was being studied. She took the first sip of her drink.

"Do you come here often?" the guest asked. He laughed, and she could smell the cloud of whiskey engulfing him.

"Let us know if there's anything we can do to make your stay more comfortable," Maria said.

"It's comfortable enough," he said, turning back towards the bar.

"Do you remember your wedding day?" he asked. "You'd never believe it, but I married the prettiest girl in my high school class."

"I don't remember," she said coolly.

Alan might chastise her later for being rude to a guest, but she stood up.

"I can't even imagine how beautiful a bride you must have been," he said.

Maria didn't look back as she carried her nearly full glass across the lobby floor to the reception desk. The man's eyes remained fixed on her, even as she settled behind the desk.

He was lucky Alan wasn't there, tucked away as he was in his office. People often asked, though typically in more veiled language, how she'd ended up married to Alan. The truth is that she didn't understand it either, nor did she try especially hard. He was a hotel owner who possessed a little of what she'd been told constituted charm, and she'd been advised by everyone around her to take his proposal seriously.

In the end, she'd followed the path of least resistance, as she so often did. She didn't regret her choice, nor did she celebrate it. She never thought much of it one way or another. Her days were spent in boredom and drink, enclosed in the glint of gold and the mellow darkness of the marble floor: unchanging beauty in which to waste her life away.

Still, her life was not without surprises. The desire Alan had shown for her the night before was unlike anything she had experienced during their years of marriage. It was as though he were seeing her in a completely new light, and the novelty had given way to intense passion.

She reflected on this as she sipped her drink. Neither Jenny nor Henry were at the reception desk yet. They often left it unmanned during the first half of the day. Alan had promised that when business was better, they would hire more staff, but Maria never minded it much. It gave her a moment to be alone in this large room, as silent as she wished to be.

Chapter Five

Henry felt an excitement he had long since assumed inaccessible as he walked down the stairs to the lobby. Though he often took the elevator, he felt that even this momentary confinement of his nervous energy might prove somehow fatal.

He didn't know what would happen when he laid eyes on Maria, but he couldn't wait to find out. Part of him was almost afraid that she knew, afraid that she would be able to sense the way he had spilled himself onto the wall at the sight of her naked body being so expertly handled by her husband.

Of course, last night had hardly been the first time he had pleasured himself to the thought of her.

Yet, when he reached the lobby, Maria was nowhere in sight. Instead, it was Jenny who greeted him.

She was wearing a blue dress which wrapped tightly around her waist, accentuating her small breasts by diminishing everything else. Her eyes were subtly made up, and there was a touch of pink tinted gloss on her lips.

The entire scene seemed odd. She was not one to give in to vanity, and her clothing typically rivalled Henry's in its dullness. Yet, here she was, looking as though she had spent a significant amount of time tending to her appearance.

There was a small flutter of anticipation in Henry's chest as he approached. Perhaps his ploy had been successful beyond anything he could have anticipated. First, Alan had offered him a private view into Maria's bedroom. Now, Jenny appeared to be sending a signal of interest.

He approached the front desk, his heart beating in his throat. His mouth had run dry, and he felt his hands shaking as he drew nearer to Jenny. He did not know what he would say, and could only hope that whatever interest he had sparked would also lead Jenny to make the first move.

Jenny had not noticed him yet, and he kept to the periphery as he closed in. Nerves made him try to delay the interaction, even by seconds.

As he drew nearer, he noticed that her eyes kept flitting across the lobby, to the bar. At first, he assumed she was keeping a disapproving eye on Maria, but soon realized that the other woman was nowhere in sight.

Instead, his eyes landed on Michael.

Michael had been at the hotel for nearly three weeks on business. When Henry checked him in, he'd seen that Michael's license listed a nearby address in New Rochelle. Given the hours he spent alone at the bar, beginning each day in the afternoon, Henry had grown to doubt that their guest was there on business. Henry was now entirely sure that Michael would be renewing his stay shortly, or booking into the hotel across the street. This was a man in exile.

On occasion, Henry would catch him glancing at Jenny. Michael's eye seemed to linger longer than a casual glance and, though she would never look back at him directly, her cheeks would flush. So, it should not have surprised Henry to find that Jenny's attempts were directed at their guest, but he felt the full pain of his quickly sprung hope dying all the same.

"Afternoon, Jenny," Henry said, trying hard to keep the fresh defeat from his voice.

"Hey," she said, her body seeming to collapse in on itself to shield from his gaze.

She was wearing perfume, something cloying and floral. It drifted finely through the air surrounding her, and awoke an almost animalistic desire in Henry, fueled by her unspoken rejection of him.

Over that afternoon and evening, he passively observed the play between Jenny and Michael: a drama of missed glances, and self-conscious adjustments of posture, hair, and clothing.

He could not even summon a righteous jealousy, given the extent of his impotence. He instead had to return in thought to his mental images of Maria from the previous night. It was strange that he had not seen her that evening, but he was relieved. If he did not know how to act around Jenny, given her flirtation with Michael, he was afraid to see how awkward he would be around his employer's wife, given the secret he was now keeping from her.

JUST AS HENRY'S SHIFT was ending, Maria came through the hotel's entrance. There was a slight sway to her movements, and she was holding two shopping bags. She wore silver earrings, which dangled a constellation of blue stones to her shoulders.

She offered him a bleary smile as she walked past Henry and toward the elevators. He couldn't imagine anything was open that late, so she must have finished her shopping some time before. It was easy to guess how she'd spent the hours between then and her arrival.

Henry followed her with brisk steps to the elevator, arriving a moment before she did, and pressing the button.

"I hope you had an enjoyable evening," he said, his tone all politeness.

She looked a little confused but shrugged.

"It was an evening," she began, but whatever thought would have followed was interrupted by the prompt arrival of the elevator.

"Sleep well, ma'am," Henry said, trying to scrape out a few more moments in her presence, even while he was counting down the seconds until he could be alone, and make his way into the secret hallway.

Alan had not said that Henry could use the mirror without invitation, but, so long as Henry knew the other man's whereabouts, he didn't see the harm in it. Besides, knowing that Maria was so nearby, so ripe for observation, would destroy any chance Henry had of a good night's sleep.

His only thought was to make the most of this window into her world, to drink every drop of the intoxicating potion he had never known before, but now could not live without.

Henry passed Alan on his way from the front desk. He was a little surprised that Alan had made no attempt at contact today, but could not explain the other man's reasoning. After all, if Henry had a wife like Maria, he would do everything he could to guard her against the intrusion of the outside world. He would be tempted to lock her away from the prying eyes of other men, to place her in a prison to which only he held the key.

Alan tilted his head toward the back office, and Henry took in a deep breath as he followed the other man, retracing the steps which would bring him to a place of privacy and the privilege of secrecy.

Alan sat down behind his desk, and Henry closed the door of the office before taking the seat opposite.

"So, did you enjoy yourself last night?" Alan asked.

Henry nodded, unsure of what exactly to say.

"Thank you," he attempted, though the words came out a little uneasily.

"Was Maria everything you'd hoped?" Alan asked, though the question hinted at something different altogether.

Henry nodded, but said nothing.

"Tell me," Alan said, leaning back a little in his chair. "What would you do with her, if you were given the chance?"

It was difficult for Henry to imagine that there was some type of offer concealed in the words. Alan's intentions were still unreadable, so Henry proceeded cautiously.

"I would put my hands on her waist," Henry began, before continuing when he was uninterrupted. "I would slide my palms upward to cup her breasts through that black nightgown she was wearing last night. I would feel her nipples with my thumbs, before bringing one of my hands between her legs."

Alan nodded and closed his eyes. "What else?"

Henry swallowed hard. "I would slip my hand into her panties, and press one of my fingers inside her."

"Is she wet?" Alan asked, his eyes still closed.

"Not yet. There's a tightness there too, because she wouldn't be ready for me. So, I massage her breast, while I continue to work my fingers inside of her. Gradually, I feel her wetness on my fingertips, and this gives me the sign that she's ready."

Alan adjusted a little in his seat, and it was not hard to guess that a growing erection must have been causing his momentary discomfort.

Henry continued. "Then, I would bend her over the foot of the bed, spread her legs a little, and tease her opening with just the tip of my cock. I would wait until she was begging me to enter her before giving her even one inch."

"What if she doesn't beg?" Alan asked, his voice slightly strained.

"She will," Henry said. "When she sees just how long and thick my cock is, it'll be everything she can do to keep herself from pushing back onto it, impaling herself on the hard, throbbing shaft."

"I admire your confidence," Alan said with a short laugh.

Henry's self-confidence was far from misplaced, but he said nothing further on the subject.

"But, let's assume she begs me for it, pleads with me to fuck her with my big cock," Henry said. "I won't make her wait long. By that point, she's got to be aching to be filled, and my duty is to her. She'll be plenty warmed up by then, so I'll thrust into her quickly, burying my cock as deep as it will go. I'll feel the width of her hips and the swell of her breasts as I fuck her from behind.

"Still, I'll want to see her face. I'll want to watch her expression as I take her completely, so I'll pull out and lay her on her back. When I reenter her, I'll get to watch the pleasure on her face, and see the jog of her breasts with every hard thrust. Best of all, I'll get to see her expression when I fill her with my cum. If I live a thousand years, I doubt I'll ever see anything as perfect as her beautiful body accepting every drop."

Alan drew in a deep breath. "How do you feel, telling me all of this?"

Henry shrugged. "I suppose as good as you do hearing it."

At this, Alan barked out a laugh of surprise. "So, you've got some guts after all. Yes, you're right: I don't mind hearing about the things you'd like to do to my wife one bit. She's a beautiful woman, but there's something beyond her superficial looks that draws men in. I can't tell you what a thrill it is to hear you describe your hopes and dreams when it comes to Maria, knowing that I'm the only one who can actually experience what you're imagining."

He paused.

"I know that must sound harsh," Alan said. "It's like I'm teasing you or something; showing you what you'll never have. But, I look at it differently. I saw what you did to the wall, just below that one-way mirror, so watching it can't have been all that painful. You can keep watching for as long as it's still enjoyable, and I hope that lasts a long time. Being able to show my wife off like that, it's a thrill I can't even begin to describe."

Henry nodded, though an uncomfortable lump had begun to form in his throat. Any mounting sense of desire he had nurtured within himself during those last few minutes had abruptly sunken, but there was nothing he could say. After all, having gained this keyhole into Maria's most private moments, he refused to let go that easily.

"Come back to the place tonight," Alan said. "I promise that if you're there at nine o'clock, you won't be disappointed by what you see."

"It's an easy promise for you to make," Henry rejoined.

Chapter Six

And it was. Henry was sure to be there by eight-thirty, and waited with bated breath as he took in the quiet scene before him. Maria was again alone in the room, though this time she did not brush her hair. The raven strands were perfectly swept and lay in waves across her golden-brown shoulders, so Henry had likely missed this part of her evening ritual.

Instead, she lay down on the bed with a book. Henry could not make out the title from where he stood, but he watched her brow crease ever so slightly as she studied the page, absorbed in the world which lay before her.

Too soon, their privacy was interrupted by Alan's entrance. Again, he stepped through the door, and Maria did not immediately acknowledge his existence. It was only after he approached her side of the bed and took the book from her hands, that she even looked in his direction.

Alan silently took her upper arm in his hand, and pulled her gently to her feet.

She was wearing the same black, silk nightgown. Alan turned her, so that she was facing Henry, and Alan stood behind her, perfectly showcasing the exotic beauty and voluptuous curves of his unsuspecting wife.

He grasped her waist, and his palms skimmed the smooth fabric as they rose to cup her breasts. He thumbed the protruding nipples lightly, as Maria bit back her breath. Her eyelids were half lowered as her husband continued his exhibitionary exploration of her body.

Alan's hand dropped to between his wife's legs, and he reached beneath the short hem of her nightgown. She was not wearing any panties, and this was the first deviation from Henry's described fantasy, which he was to helplessly watch played out before him.

Still, the absence of material did not stop Alan. He slid a finger inside her, and Henry registered the slight gasp of discomfort, and the way Maria shifted. It seemed she was not yet warmed up enough to allow comfortable entry.

Still, Alan massaged her breast, kneaded the full curve, while his other hand pressed its thick digits inside of her, resuming an unsteady pace until a yielding wetness had grown within her, and Henry could see her relaxing into the penetrative touch.

Henry knew what was coming next, and he unzipped his pants, removing his hard cock from the confines of his clothing, only seconds before Alan did the same. Henry knew that his own size was more impressive, and he grasped the shaft with a level of confidence, beginning to stroke his length as he watched Maria through the mirror.

Alan guided Maria to the foot of the bed, where he bent her over, stepping aside a little to leave her in full view of their hidden spectator. Alan kneaded the flesh of his wife's rounded ass, lightly slapping it, though only the faintest sound made it through the glass.

Henry stroked harder as he took in every detail of her submissive body, enjoying the sight of her bent over before her husband, imagining that she would succumb similarly to his pleasure, if only he could find a way to turn her to his will.

Alan pressed his cock against her entrance and thrust forward. Now, Henry could only make out the side of her body as it was rammed from behind by Alan's aggressive advance. Soon enough, Alan pulled out, flipped Maria onto her back, and stepped between her legs. He reentered her, and his thrusts found a fast, steady rhythm, sinking deep into her body.

Henry's stroking of his own cock became idle as his mind wandered to what would come next. There was a sudden bitterness to the scene before him, knowing that soon he would watch helplessly as Alan filled Maria with ejaculate. Henry tried to distract himself from this eventuality by focusing on the way Alan's hips slammed against Maria, the way the side of her breast bounced back and forth with the impact.

Henry was unsuccessful in this, and found that he could not orgasm quickly enough to avoid seeing Alan finish deep inside his wife. When Alan pulled out and Maria sat up, it was with a level of despair that Henry watched a trickle of cum leak from her and onto the bedspread.

His own cock was still hard, but he had lost the desire to pleasure himself any further. Instead, he numbly watched the two prepare for bed. The lights were switched off, but the glow of the emergency exit sign illuminated their reclining silhouettes.

In time, Henry's eyes adjusted to the low level of light, and he watched as the two slept. He could see the curve of Maria's hips and breasts as she lay on her side. He could see the gentle shift of her bosom as she breathed deeply.

Just when Henry was considering leaving, Maria sat up. Her hands were in her lap, and the nightgown had come down a little to reveal the full swell of her breasts. Henry felt a thrill run through him, and his hand grasped his cock again, beginning to administer long, powerful strokes.

Maria ran her hand through her hair, and looked up at the ceiling, seemingly in boredom. She adjusted the straps of her nightgown, and Henry allowed his imagination to take hold again. He imagined what his cock would look like between those two breasts, how warm she would be. He tried to picture himself sinking his considerable length between her legs, inch by thick inch, and feeling the soft, warm wetness engulf him.

He came, this time into his hand. While he tried to clean himself up a little, he watched as she retrieved something small from her bedside table. He considered leaving, his voyeurism having reached the desired conclusion, but he decided to stay.

She replaced whatever she had taken from the nightstand, and turned to the other side, so that she was sitting beside her sleeping husband. Henry couldn't see exactly what she did, but he saw her hand near Alan's face, as the other man's body began to twist uncomfortably, though he never seemed to wake.

After a minute or two of this same, strange action, Maria returned to her side of the bed, and lay down, facing the wall.

HENRY PUZZLED OVER what he had seen as he made his way back to his bedroom, but found he had no more clarity than he had started with.

As he lay down, he allowed his mind to drift. It went, as it so often did, to his childhood. His father had been a strong man. Henry had never seen him afraid of anyone or anything, and he'd always known that he was a disappointment to his father. After all, the elder man was impossibly strong, and wouldn't have wanted someone like Henry as a son. So, from an early age, Henry was twisted from within, and masking weakness had became his greatest strength.

It was not until one morning, when Henry saw a pharmacy bottle by the side of his parents' bed, that he realized his father was not the man he had built him up to be. His mother was a beautiful woman, and the fact that her husband needed *that* reduced him to a pathetic weakling in Henry's mind. After all, Henry knew that he'd never have experienced that failing if it were him. He had thought about it all that day, imagining his mother's countless disappointments. Before that fateful morning, he had supposed that having him as her son had been her primary regret.

That night, so many years ago, beneath the darkness, Henry had felt his hand traveling lower, his fingers meeting the proof of his hard manhood: proof that there were ways in which he was stronger than his father. The rigid flesh reassured him, and he let it go limp in his hand, engaging every ounce control. He fell asleep, still grasping himself and drawing security from the embrace of his own flesh.

And now, he had his father to thank for the fact that he could not go to sleep without completing this ritual. He could not release himself from consciousness without feeling his own rigid hardness, without examining the proof of his manhood, reminding himself that he was more a man than was his father, that he could give a woman like his mother what she deserved.

Henry had spent time imagining the moment of his conception, making himself sick imagining her degradation, forced to placate a man who could not perform as nature had intended him to.

Whatever else, Henry knew himself to be superior in that respect.

That night, he slipped into a restless sleep, replaying the events of the night before, and only emphasizing his own sense of helplessness.

Chapter Seven

In the months leading up to her discovery, Maria had felt a change in her body. It was difficult to quantify in any real way; it was a physical sense of unease, creeping and minute. Then, she had cut her finger. It was a paper cut from one of the hundreds of white sheets which populated the reception desk.

She'd nearly pressed the cut to her lip, when she noticed the way the red liquid was eating through the paper. It made it through the page, and then a layer of varnished wood below, before neutralizing. She wiped up the remaining mixture with a tissue, and the bleeding quickly stopped. She then explored this phenomenon for the rest of the day. She made small incisions all over her body, and was surprised to find that only healthy, fresh, red blood seeped from the shallow cuts. Each time, she pressed the red droplets to her tongue, but was met only by the metallic taste of blood. Finally. she used a needle to prick her fingertip. Almost immediately, the blood began to corrode the metal.

She watched the process with a curiosity she hadn't felt in years. She didn't know at the time what this meant, nor did she know that within weeks, she would cover her fingertips with scars: white lines intersecting in a web of pain, drawn small across her skin.

It wasn't long before the strange process had moved from the world of pure oddity to that of cold-blooded application. Perhaps this too was just another curiosity spurred by boredom. All she knew was that the first time she cut her finger and slid the wet digit into her sleeping husband's mouth, she felt a kind of amusement. She had then taken to spilling more blood into his open mouth, and down his throat. He never woke, but she could see the damage wrought, smell the way her blood corroded his living flesh.

After a time, this strange thrill had become her will to live. She numbed herself throughout the interim, the daylit hours no longer holding any appeal.

She began every morning in a desperate fugue, her every fiber stretched toward the first drink of the day, the tonic she needed to make it from her room until she could return to her bed. Hurting her husband was the only satisfaction left to her.

Chapter Eight

Maria was the first person Henry saw that day. He was heading out to lunch, before his shift began, and he passed her in the lobby. Maria looked tired and, though she looked at him, she did not nod or say hello. He was used to this, and offered her a small, tight-lipped smile.

He wanted to do more, but it somehow didn't feel right. He could feel the adrenaline racing through his veins at just the sight of her, so he made his way from the hotel as quickly as he could. On the way out, he nearly ran into Jenny, who was carrying a few shopping bags. Jenny, like Henry, lived in the hotel, and was walking quickly enough that it seemed she was intent on avoiding an encounter with anyone she knew.

"I'm so sorry," she stammered, when she realized with whom she had nearly collided.

"No problem," Henry said. "Can I help you with anything?"

He glanced at the bags she was carrying, and quickly recognized the branding of a few nearby lingerie, cosmetics, and clothing stores among the number she had looped over her upper arms.

"I'm fine, thanks," she said, stepping past him. "See you later."

Given the way she had dressed the day before, and the way she had seemed to avoid looking too long at Michael, where he sat at the bar, it was clear these purchases were just another part of her passive flirtation with their long-term guest.

Henry stewed over this development as he choked down a sandwich. He sat on a park bench, staring absently at the people as they walked by. His eye would occasionally linger a little longer on beautiful young women as they passed, but there was a further interest generated when couples would walk by. He watched the interlaced hands, the trading of glances, and flirtatious smiles with a growing resentment. He was as invisible to them as he was to Maria and Jenny.

When he returned to the hotel to begin his shift, it was with a stalling anger that each step was controlled. Jenny was already behind the front desk, punctual as always. She was wearing a new dress, made of a soft, rose-pink fabric. He noticed that her breasts sat higher, a little more pronounced. Her makeup was subtler than it had been the day before, as though she had been given a new level of guidance. As his eyes traveled across her body, he noticed the absence of a panty line beneath the sheer, clinging fabric.

There was a pointedness to the way Jenny would avoid looking toward the bar, where Michael sat in his usual seat. Maria was at the opposite end of the bar, clutching a tall glass in her elegant hand.

Henry couldn't help himself. He was desperate to cause Jenny some kind of pain.

"So, the things you bought," he began, noting the way Jenny's eyes flicked nervously towards him, "they're for him, right? You want that guy to notice you."

Jenny's mouth opened, but no words came out. It seemed she was too stunned by the bluntness of his observation to speak, and Henry quickly overcame the silence.

"If he didn't like you the way you were," he said, looking her over from head to foot, "well, just how long do you think you can keep this up? Is this a whole new Jenny we're getting?"

Her cheeks flamed red, and she looked down. Tears had already sprung to her eyes, and she kept her gaze fixed on the floor, as she raced from the reception desk to the ladies' restroom, just down the hall.

Henry did not know why, but he followed her. Perhaps the time spent impotently watching the subject of his obsession be defiled night after night had pent up a ruthless energy within him.

He swung open the restroom door.

Jenny was bent over the sink, pressing her face into the little water she held between two cupped hands. She looked up, obviously shocked to see Henry stride towards her in the women's room. The water streamed from her face down her chest, causing the fabric of her dress to become nearly translucent.

"Henry, you can't be here," she said, taking a step back as he neared.

"I'm sorry," he said

Her back hit the wall, and her hands became small fists. "Henry, you should—"

"I just...I wanted to say that I was sorry," Henry said, standing awkwardly in the middle of the room, taking in the rigidity of Jenny's body, and the way she hadn't moved from the place furthest from him.

"We should get back," Jenny said finally.

"I don't know what came over me," Henry continued, ignoring her hint. "It just made me sorry to see him ignore you, because I care about you. I care about you very much, and I want to protect you."

Something in Jenny's face softened, and she took a small step forward from the wall.

"It's okay," she said. "I forgive you."

She stepped a little closer, and pulled him into a hug.

"It's nice that you want to protect me," she said, though her words were a little stilted. "But I think we should get back."

Henry nodded, before walking from the restroom. He settled in the lobby, where Maria and Michael were still seated at the bar, seemingly unnoticing of Henry and Jenny's momentary absence.

When Jenny joined him at the front desk, she had washed her face. She seemed somehow plain without the makeup. She had done her best to dry her clothing, but there was still a dampness to the way the dress material clung to her breasts.

Henry was surprised that she had not returned to her room to change and reapply makeup, but perhaps her mind was no longer on Michael. Whatever happened, Henry would do his best to make sure her attentions never returned to the guest perpetually seated at the bar.

Chapter Nine

That evening, Henry found himself in the hallway, staring through the mirror at the unsuspecting Maria. This time, he was not invited by Alan. He had been avoiding his employer throughout the day, afraid that he would snap, if prompted to describe another sexual fantasy which would be acted out in front of him. He had never imagined being cuckolded by his own fantasies, but this is what had happened only the night before.

Alan was nowhere in sight, and Henry's ears were tuned to every sound around him. He was half afraid that the older man had made his way into the hallway, to see if Henry had become emboldened enough to act as voyeur in his own right.

But no sounds came.

Maria had only just entered the bedroom. The gentle sway in her step reminded Henry of the hours he had watched her seated at the bar, her drinks refilled with a metronomic consistency. She must have had five gin and tonics just during the time Henry was observing her.

She slipped off her high-heeled shoes and set them down by the door. Her hair had been tied up nicely at the nape of her neck, and she let the inky tresses down in a single, fluid motion.

She unzipped her dress, and let the fabric fall to the ground around her feet. She stepped free and picked up the article of clothing, folding it over the back of the arm chair in the corner. She stood in the middle of the room, wearing matching burgundy lace panties and bra. She stared at the door for a moment, and it seemed as though her entire body collapsed inwardly. Her shoulders were sunken, creating a contagious sense of hollowness within her hidden viewer.

Maria sat down on the edge of the bed, and buried her head in her hands. Her hair fell in waves across her bent arms, and she pressed her forehead hard into her palms, hard enough that even from where Henry stood, he could see the trembling pressure exacted in this solitary moment.

Her breast rose and fell with deep, controlled breaths, and her fingers tightened around her buried face. In an instant, she was standing again, her body relaxed, and attuned to her environment. She went to her bedside table, opened the drawer, looked inside, and closed it again.

She sat down and stood back up almost immediately. She seemed nervous, and this energy shone through even the drunken dampening to which she had subjected herself. Henry watched with fascination the little, restless movements which possessed her as she walked across the room: fidgeting as she paced unsteadily, her bare feet finding their mark after the occasional falter.

Henry noticed that the bedding had been changed. It was no longer the decadent black and gold cover. Instead, there was a black quilt blanket in its place.

The door opened, and Alan walked through. His brow was creased, and he gave only a cursory glance to his nearly naked wife, who had frozen in place the moment he crossed the threshold.

He said something as he loosened his tie, and she looked up. He seemed to remember himself, but his movements were short and forceful as he undid the top few buttons of his shirt.

It occurred to Henry that there might be a simple explanation for Alan's apparent mood, and he stepped away from the mirror. He pulled his cell phone out of his pocket, and was greeted by the sight of nearly twenty messages from Alan.

He scrolled through the notifications, and saw a monologue which began with an inquiry regarding Henry's plans for the evening, and an invitation to the private show which Henry had been enjoying over the past few days. After fifteen unanswered messages, the language became fraught, with Alan expressing a sense that Henry was unsatisfied, or that he had taken advantage of the couple's private moments before losing interest.

There was even a message which speculated that Henry was trying to have an affair with Maria. The final text, however, was an abusive line expressing Henry's forthcoming termination.

Henry's heart began pounding, and he tried to press back the tears which threatened to fall. He typed out a response, apologizing for the delay, and insisting that he would be there, and that he had no lack of appreciation for the world Alan had allowed him to enter.

Letting out a breath he did not realize he had been holding, Henry returned to the mirror, where he saw Alan looking at his own cell phone. The expression on his employer's face softened a little, and Alan set the phone down on his nightstand without responding.

Maria said something to Alan, which Henry could not hear, but a grin spread across the other man's face. He glanced at the mirror behind which Henry was hiding, and sent another message.

Are you there?

Henry's phone lit up blue, and he stepped back from the mirror.

Yes

He typed the word quickly, before resuming his vigil. Now, Alan was grinning fully as he looked his wife over. Maria went to the closet beside the mirror, briefly drifting out of sight, before returning to the bedside, holding strips of silken cloth, knotted together.

She sat down on the bed, and began gently unknotting the ties. Alan, meanwhile, undressed himself and lay down on the bed. Maria knelt by his side, and tied his nearest wrist to the bed post, she moved to his ankle, before knotting the opposite wrist and ankle.

Alan lay naked and tied to the bed, supine and flat except for his heavy, jutting manhood. He grinned as he took in Maria's movement around the room.

To Henry's surprise, the woman did not undress. Instead, she came to sit by Alan's side. She stroked his hair as she spoke to him, though Henry could not make out the words coming from her mouth.

Maria then opened the bedside table and removed a small knife from the drawer. As soon as Alan laid eyes on the blade, he began thrashing, trying to free himself from the restraints.

Henry's heart began pounding as he took in the scene. Thinking quickly, he pulled his phone out, switched off the flash, and took a picture. The image clearly showed Maria over the bound body of her husband, wielding the small blade.

When he lowered his phone, Henry realized that he was most struck by the smallness of the blade. He could only imagine how many cuts it would take to end the life of his employer.

Maria straddled her husband's waist, still clutching the handle of the knife. Her back was facing Henry, but he could see her oblique reflection in the mirror of her vanity table. She was still speaking, but her words were inaudible.

To his surprise, she did not strike her husband with the knife. Instead, she ran the blade of the knife against her own hand, slicing across her fingers. Blood began to flow, and she pressed her palm over her husband's mouth. Alan began thrashing with a violence his previous attempts to free himself had not possessed. The bed shook with the force of his movements, and he nearly bucked Maria from the bed, but she gripped his throat with her other hand, pressing the bleeding digits back to his mouth.

Alan's chest heaved and shuddered, but in time, he stilled. When Maria moved from where she had been sitting on his stomach, he could see a bloody fluid leaking from the man's mouth.

Maria touched her fingers to Alan's wrist, holding them there for what felt like an excruciating length of time. She then reached into her bedside table, and removed what appeared to be a compact mirror.

She opened the clamshell compact, and held the small reflective surface a few inches from Alan's mouth and nose. Seemingly satisfied with the results of this experiment, she shut the compact, replaced it in the bedside table drawer, and began untying the strips of cloth.

It was then that Henry understood why the bedding had been changed. Maria began rolling the duvet around Alan's body, before dropping the wrapped corpse to the floor. She dragged it into the bathroom, where Henry could no longer see her.

Henry had watched a man die. It was not the death of a good man, not by any stretch of the imagination, but Henry felt a strange electricity running through him. He felt sick to his stomach, but there was a level of excitement at thinking that he had witnessed a moment Maria had never meant to be observed, far beyond the voyeurism of the previous days. He alone shared this secret with her, and it was a bond he did not fully understand.

Not yet.

Chapter Ten

Misery.

This was the word on Maria's tongue when she had awoken that morning, and it was for the sake of nothing less than absolute, abject misery that she would enact the plan which had been formed in her mind. It was the same plan which explained the cheap blanket that was kept tucked in the back of her closet.

It was misery that forced her hand. She had never wanted to take a life, but she'd become increasingly convinced that she had been compromised in some way. It was a sneaking suspicion that resulted from the way her husband had been acting toward her, the strange spring in his step over the past several days, and the way he seemed to be paying true attention to her. She knew that he did not believe her to be worthy of his undivided attention, which meant there was some hidden factor at work in his mind.

Her small acts of violence, committed when he lay in his sleep, were no longer enough. She needed him dead.

So, around midday, she had returned to their room and changed the bed. She stuffed the beautiful bedspread in the back of her closet, where the other had resided until that moment. She winced, seeing the ornate fabric wrinkled and crushed, but she would do her best to rectify that later.

She finally understood her purpose.

She returned to the lobby bar and ordered a gin and tonic. She kept drinking through to the evening. This time, though, it was not to numb herself, nor was it to summon the courage she would need to end a life. Instead, it was a celebration of what was to come, no different than an ancient army engaging in revelry before the day of battle.

By the time she had returned to the room, Maria was forgetting her urgency. Still, she went through the meager preparations left to her, ever on the verge of drunkenness while awaiting her husband's return.

As soon as Alan stepped through the door, Maria could sense a shift in his mood. While the previous days had shown the man to be inexplicably jovial, now he seemed troubled and kept looking at his phone. A message lit up the screen as he was beginning to undress, and his countenance abruptly shifted. He looked around the room and his eyes landed on her, as though finally seeing her.

It was then that the nearly suffocated rage within her chest found its breath again, and she assessed her husband with a predatory eye.

"Do you want to try something a little different tonight?" she asked, masking her anger behind a drunken, leisurely smile.

Alan grinned wide, again looking at a place in the room far from where she stood.

"Like what?" he asked.

"Something we haven't done since our anniversary last year," she practically purred. "It's been that long since you've let me take control."

Maria walked to the closet, where she retrieved the silky ties. She had placed them there a week ago, and she had to smile as she thought of the ways in which that one closet had become her own personal, large scale murder kit.

Alan had already undressed by the time she rejoined him at the bed, and his cock was hard. Maria offered him her most helplessly lascivious smile as she tied the first knot at his wrist.

She stayed silent, but offered him those same lingering gazes, pretending in moments to be shy, almost nervous about what was happening. She laughed a little as she retied the knot at his right ankle. She would never let on that she had been practicing tying impossibly strong knots with those same ties for the past several days.

Alan watched her eagerly from his position on the bed, waiting for her to undress. Still, she could not help but feel his attention was somewhere far from her.

She sat down beside him, still clothed, and touched his cheek lightly.

"Alan, how long have we been married?" she asked.

"Too long," he laughed.

It was the same joke he had made since their honeymoon.

Maria reached down and touched his temple, before running her fingers through his hair.

"And yet," she said, "I can't help but think it isn't long enough. Maybe if we knew each other, truly knew each other, the small releases of pent-up anger, resentment, and pain would be enough. They were for a time, you know."

Alan's expression morphed to one of confusion.

"What are you talking about, small releases?" he asked.

"Oh, nothing," Maria said, still stroking his hair gently. "It's just like letting a little pressure off, you know? Maybe if there was something real to sustain us, we could find some kind of equilibrium."

"Maria, untie me," he said, his eyes widening.

Instead, she reached into the bedside table was retrieved the knife. It was the same knife which had inflicted countless small wounds since her discovery and, though this was the first time Alan was seeing the blade, it was far from the first time the knife had entered their marital bed.

He began to struggle to free himself, but the knots only tightened as he tugged against them. His hands grew purple with the stilled blood in his veins, but he only tried harder to free himself, strangling his appendages.

Maria straddled her husband, and there was an odd melancholy as she realized that it was the last time she would have this man between her legs.

She took the knife, and drew the blade across the inside of her fingers. She had calculated the point of incision exactly, so that there would be a copious flow of blood, but avoid permanent injury to herself.

Her hand began profusely bleeding, and she pressed the wounds to his lips, forcing the corrosive blood into his mouth and down his throat. She had never experimented with even a fraction of this amount of blood, and the difference in the effect was immediately apparent.

She could hear a popping, sizzling sound as her blood made contact with his flesh. He began writhing, no longer trying in any deliberate way to free himself. A clear, foamy fluid began spilling from his mouth, but she only forced more of her own blood down his throat.

In time, he stilled. She could see the massive damage wrought as she tipped his head back and forth. She pressed her fingers to his wrist, searching for some stubborn pulse, but after a few minutes, she could find nothing.

As a final test, she retrieved the diamond encrusted compact which Alan had given her for her birthday the previous year. She set the mirror an inch below his nose, holding her breath even as she searched for a symptom of his own.

When no sign came, she replaced the unfogged mirror in the bedside table, and quickly began the work for which the room had been prepared. She wrapped Alan in the blanket, before dragging him onto the floor and into the bathroom.

He was much heavier than she had imagined him to be, and it was a struggle to get him past the threshold. However, once she was in the bathroom, on the frictionless floor, it became much easier to drag him.

When he was finally on the far side of the sleek floor, she made the phone call. She wouldn't say that it had been easy to find someone to dispose of the man, but it hadn't been too difficult either.

Right on time, there was a knock at the door. She was greeted by the sight of a scruffy-bearded man wearing a baseball cap and pushing a hotel cart. He entered without a word, pushed the cart to the bathroom, loaded his morbid cargo, and departed just as quickly.

Maria was now left alone in the room. She went into the closet and retrieved the black and gold bedspread. She laid it out on the canopy bed, enjoying the emptiness before her. She used her palms to iron out the little wrinkles, and she tucked the edges neatly, focusing every ounce of her attention on this small, yet infinitely meaningful task.

She lay down on top of the cool, silken fabric and allowed her body to relax. She could practically breathe her solitude, and the years ahead had once again assumed the glow of endless possibility.

Her cell phone buzzed on the bedside table, and she languidly reached for it. There was a message from an unknown number and she opened it to find no words.

Only a picture.

Chapter Eleven

Who is this?

A fair question.

Alan had shared both his and his wife's contact information with the new employees, though Henry was sure this was without Maria's knowledge. He had never used the number before, though that wasn't to say he hadn't been tempted. During some of those long nights, with nothing but his own hand to keep him company, he had contemplated sending her proof of his neglected manhood. Yet, it seemed he was as afraid to initiate interaction over the phone as he was in person.

He tried to decide what to write back. He could only imagine how frightened and confused she must be. An unknown number had sent a photo of her straddling her husband while wielding a knife. Henry could hardly make rational sense of everything he had seen after that moment, which was now frozen in time on his phone. Yet, he was sure that he had witnessed a murder. He did not know what the method of execution could possibly be considered, and it was largely out of this confusion that he decided to send the photo.

Who do you think this is?

He responded, wincing at the weakness of the text on the page.

Henry

His anticipated game of cat and mouse had been cut ruthlessly short. She had barely hesitated.

Yes.

He responded in the simple affirmative. There was no doubt that she was grappling for the upper hand. All that was left for him to do was try to avoid showing his surprise.

I'm coming.

The phone slipped from his hands and her final message stared up at him from the floor. He took a moment to process this, but soon forced himself to action.

He tried to straighten up the room, before rushing to the bathroom to brush his hair and splash water on his face. The droplets streamed down his sharp cheekbones and defined jaw. He had to admit that the reflection staring back at him was not without a certain level of attractiveness, but it was something he had never been able to effectively utilize. It would have been better given to someone else.

Still, there was no time to waste. Maria would be outside his door shortly, and his desire to make a good impression as she reassessed him in earnest was crushing.

He changed into a button-down shirt and jeans, before sitting down on the bed, feeling frustrated in his solitary awkwardness.

There was a knock at the door: a series of three taps.

Henry rose and answered.

Maria stood there, wearing a red dress, and wrapped in a black trench coat, which only lightly brushed her body as she stepped into his hotel room.

"So, you know," she said.

"I do," Henry answered.

"How did you take the picture?" she asked.

Henry noticed that her hand was bandaged, and that she had refreshed her makeup after the struggle with Alan. The end of her ponytail was wet, so he assumed she had also taken a shower.

"Your husband showed me where to stand," he answered simply.

Maria let out a sharp laugh.

"So, he was living out some kind of fantasy at my expense. I'd assumed this was more or less the case, but I hadn't imagined it was quite this involved."

"How did you know it was me?" Henry asked without missing a beat.

"Who else would it have been?" Maria answered tiredly. "I could see the change in dynamic between the two of you after the incident with the pornographic book. It seems my husband found a way to work you into his designs."

Henry nodded.

"But you agreed, and I doubt it was just because you were worried about getting fired," she continued.

"I wanted to see you," Henry said, clasping her forearm, and drawing her towards him. "I can't tell you how jealous I became watching the two of you together. All I could think about was how much better I could treat you, how safe and satisfied you would feel if those were my arms, not his, wrapped around you at the end of the day."

Maria looked him over with an unreadable expression. She took in a short breath, before freeing herself from his hold, and sitting down on the edge of the bed.

"What do you want from me?" she asked.

He had to admire her directness throughout this interaction, from the moment she responded to the photo. Then again, he knew she had killed her husband, so he supposed the time for veiled language had long since passed.

"What do you think would be a fair trade for my silence?" he asked, hoping to match her candor.

Her expression softened, and she looked him in the eye from where she sat on the bed. Her head was angled toward him, as though she were trying to catch his meaning.

He didn't imagine that understanding his desires was particularly difficult. Sure enough, her eyes widened.

"That's all it would take? Do you really care for me that much?" Maria asked. "You must know that I have money. I could even make you a gift of the hotel. You could begin a new chapter of your life here."

"I don't want those things," Henry said.

"Don't you?" she continued. "I sold my soul for those things long ago."

"And look at where it led you," Henry interjected. "Can you promise me that I would be happier than you were?"

"Yes," she said.

"But it's not what I want," Henry said.

He reached forward and took her chin in his hand, then he stooped down to kiss her lips. Her mouth was frozen against his, but after a moment of hesitation, she yielded to him, relaxing and returning the kiss.

"I want you," he breathed against her neck.

She looked up at him with eyes as wide as they were cunning.

"Then, you can have me. However, within one week, you'll wish you'd asked for anything else," she murmured.

MARIA'S TRENCH COAT slipped from her shoulders and pooled on the bedspread, though the garment still clung stubbornly to her hips.

Henry slipped his fingertips under the red fabric at Maria's shoulder, and slid the material down over her arms, until she was naked from the waist up. He was pleased to see that she was wearing a new bra. This one was made of sheer black lace, and he could see the light brown of her nipples through the sheer fabric. They began to harden in the cold air, and Henry hungrily took in the sight before him.

He reached down to cup one of her breasts. He squeezed lightly against the fullness of her flesh, feeling the soft lace material against far softer skin.

His erection was growing, and his hard member strained against the confines of his jeans. Maria's eyes drifted downward, settling on the bulge which indicated the arousal she had long since inspired in him.

Maria reached up after only a moment's hesitation, and felt the length of the hard cock in front of her. She opened her thighs and tugged at his belt loop, pulling Henry forward to stand between her legs. She unzipped his pants and freed his erection.

At just the briefest brush of Maria's fingers against his cock, Henry felt as though he might lose every ounce of himself in that moment. He forced himself to remain in control and, as if to demonstrate this, he reached down and gave his cock a few long, slow strokes, bringing the jutting member to within inches of Maria's lips.

It seemed this was all the encouragement she needed. Her red lips parted, and Henry watched, almost powerless, as the tip of his cock disappeared between them.

He was much larger than her husband had been, so Henry waited patiently, as Maria gradually drew more of him into her mouth with every movement of her lips over his shaft.

A shiver ran down his spine as he allowed his eyes to wander over her breasts, and down her stomach, knowing that there was only one place still concealed from him, but he liked that. It gave him something to unwrap in the coming days. He would force himself to slow, and enjoy the gradual escalation as his blackmail scheme bore fruit.

Her lips and tongue moved with undeniable expertise, drawing sensations from his body which he had never experienced before. He felt suddenly strong, powerful beyond anything he could explain.

When he reached his climax, he was too intimidated to even touch her. His fingers ached to feel her body, but he could only summon the strength to touch her hair. Feeling the soft strands felt almost too intimate.

He straightened his clothes, and was surprised to see that the look on Maria's face was not one of anger, revulsion, or even sadness. Instead, there was a curiosity in her eyes, as though she were making a study of him.

He felt suddenly exposed, and he cast his eyes down, trying in subtle ways to skirt her sudden, intense attention.

"I'm sorry," he blurted out, his eyes still locked on the floor.

To his surprise, Maria rose from the edge of the bed. She ran her finger down his chest, her nail catching on each button and causing them to jump.

"No, you're not," she whispered against his neck. "I've seen the way you watch me. I can feel the lust radiating off of you. You're not sorry, not now, but you will be."

She pressed a hard kiss to his mouth, and he could faintly taste blood, as his lips were crushed against his own teeth.

Maria fixed her dress, and draped the trench coat back over her shoulders. She offered Henry a small, vaguely flirtatious wave as she left the room, slamming the door shut loudly behind her.

Chapter Twelve

The night didn't bring even a minute of sleep to Henry. He was lost in thought, replaying every moment with Maria. He remembered the way she had taken him into her mouth, expertly working his member. He could feel the dribble of precum created at the thought, and tried to steer his thoughts into more neutral territory.

He only succeeded in fixating on Maria's words of warning. He was hardly surprised to learn that his attention toward her had not gone unnoticed, though he had considered her frequent drunken state to be some kind of protection against a return of attention.

It seemed he had been a voyeur since the moment he'd laid eyes on her, but this status had only been cemented upon the invitation of her husband. He supposed that Alan had similarly noticed the study Henry had made of Maria, but Henry spared only a moment of thought on the dead man, before returning to the subject of his widow.

Instead of waking to the sunlight, Henry's restless consciousness gradually registered the lightening sky, and it was with an anxious weariness that he progressed hours later from his bed, where he had spent an uncomfortable night fully clothed.

He started his shift early, too nervous to eat or drink anything. He was consumed by thoughts that would not relent, but the strongest among them was the thought that he had now known something of Maria, of the sexual delight she offered. The idea that he might have tasted such incredible, undeniable pleasure only to have it taken from him was crushing in its darkness.

He must have been visibly distracted, because Jenny gave him a frown when she arrived for her shift.

"You look a little rumpled," she said, her eyes indicating the wrinkled clothes in which he had fruitlessly chased sleep.

Her cheeks colored at her own impoliteness, though Henry could hardly imagine why. He had practically forced himself on her only the other day, so if anyone should be mired in shame, it was undoubtedly him.

Jenny was wearing a light layer of makeup and her clothing was new, or at least an outfit Henry had never seen before. She was dressed in a sheer, nearly transparent white blouse, and he could see the faint silhouette of a light blue bra. The blouse was tucked into a gray skirt with pleats at the left hip. The skirt came to a place about six inches above her knee, and all that Henry could think about was bending her over the reception desk, pulling her panties to the side, and fucking her senseless. It seemed that the restless, weary energy Maria had instilled in him was seeking an outlet, and Jenny seemed just as ripe as she had the day before.

His possession of Maria in some form or another had awoken a hungry greed within him. He wanted Maria, he wanted Jenny, he wanted a goddamn harem of women who would shed blood, sweat, and tears to please him absolutely. Once, he had begged for a morsel, but now he wanted every last crumb the world could offer.

Maria exited the elevator, now wearing a black dress, but with the same trench coat draped over her shoulders. She glanced dismissively at Henry, though looked a little longer at Jenny, before making her way to the bar. Within seconds, her fingers were wrapped around a gin and tonic, and the smudge of her lipstick graced the condensation coated glass.

It seemed some things would remain the same.

Yet one thing was different. This time, she was actually talking to Michael. It did not seem to be particularly engrossing conversation, and Henry noticed that she would look toward the place where he and Jenny stood, but only every so often. It seemed her focus was on something beyond her surroundings, beyond even the conversation she was having with their perennial guest.

Henry was almost afraid to find out why she was suddenly so talkative. She glanced in his direction, and flipped her hair over her shoulder, baring her smooth, bronze neck to his sight in a way that was openly invitational.

After a short time, she stood up from where she was seated at the bar, and made her way to the back office. Henry had counted three drinks, though the slight sway in her walk made him think it was most likely more.

"Henry, can I speak to you?" she asked as she walked to the office. She beckoned him with a single, crooked finger.

He immediately stepped away from the desk, peeling himself in degrees from his place in view of the public, following her to a hidden realm. There was a hesitancy to the way in which he pursued. He had, for this brief moment, held all the cards, and experienced delights beyond anything he might have wished. It felt tenuous, as though a single word from her ruby-painted lips could burst the hopeful bubble in which he had placed himself.

Maria was already seated behind Alan's desk when Henry stepped into the room. Her high-heel clad feet were crossed at the corner of the desk, allowing Henry full view of what was hidden beneath her dress. His eye traced the line of her calf to her inner thigh, before finally resting on the black lace panties, which showcased the curvature of her buttocks and the cleft between her legs.

Henry almost immediately felt the pulse of blood in his cock, and Maria glanced at the hint of the growing erection within his pants. She smiled, baring the tips of her white teeth as she looked him over.

"So, it seems our Jenny has a little crush on you," she laughed lightly. She gestured for him to sit down, and Henry complied immediately.

He tried not to appear too confused by her statement, so he again masked his lack of understanding beneath silence.

Maria smiled and, though there was an edge to her expression, it was not at all unkind.

"It could be amusing," she said. "Jenny's a sweet girl, though a little meek for my liking. I'd imagine you've thought more than once in your life about having two women at the same time."

Henry nodded.

"Have you ever thought about having sex with me and Jenny?" she continued.

Again, Henry could only nod.

"I think it might be an interesting way to enliven this little blackmail scheme you hatched, but also a challenge. Do you think you are capable of seducing Jenny?" she asked.

"I don't know," Henry said.

And it was true. He could not answer yes honestly. They had shared that moment in the bathroom, but the force with which he approached her could not exactly be considered seduction.

Still, there was the way Jenny had been looking at him since that moment. The way she was dressed and made up, and the fact that she did not seem to spend as much of her attention on the man at the bar after whom she had been almost openly lusting for weeks.

"I do," Maria said, stroking her hand beneath her knee. "You can seduce her. You can bring her into our bed, but start simple. Just make your attraction known. Show her that you see her for the beautiful, complex, sweet woman that she is, and she should be wet clay in your hands. Soon enough, you'll be molding her to your own particular brand of depravity."

Henry's heart raced. The prospect was undeniably thrilling. He had only once or twice entertained the image of himself with the two women. In truth, it seemed too painful, as though he were torturing himself with this far-fetched notion. Instead, he had focused on fantasies involving one of the two women at a time. It was a step closer to his realm of possibility, and this had lessened the heartache, but only somewhat.

"Where do I begin?" Henry asked, the weakness of his words almost immediately searing his tongue.

Maria looked him over with an expression that nearly resembled pity, before it morphed to one of maternal guidance.

"I would start by asking her for a drink," she said. "It may sound simple, but a girl like Jenny, as pretty as she might be, doesn't get too much direct attention. A little force behind your words will do wonders for her."

Henry nodded, though it still sounded too good to be true.

"But, how does a drink with Jenny help bring her into our bed?" he asked.

Maria laughed lightly at his use of the words 'our bed'. "You let me worry about the next steps. Begin by presenting yourself to her, and making her view you seriously as a romantic prospect."

She paused, before continuing. "Do you still have that book? You know, the one that I'm guessing began the special activities my husband introduced you to?"

Henry nodded, but a flush colored his cheeks at her mention of his fumbling cry for attention. Though it had only been a few days earlier, it felt as though that book, and even the man Henry had been, existed in a lifetime apart from his own.

"I have the book," he said.

Maria smiled. "Bring it on your date with Jenny. Just put it on the table, but make sure you're confident when you do. Your weakness poisoned your positioning of the book earlier. You are no longer begging for someone to look at you like a man. Now, you're demanding her attention as someone who can initiate her into a world of sensuality that she has only imagined."

Henry sat there, hesitating. Everything he had ever wanted was being offered to him, and seemingly gladly so, yet there were lingering doubts in his mind. The doubts were no longer those of the 'too good to be true' variety. Instead, his doubts were solidly in himself as a candidate for sexual interest.

Again, Maria seemed to anticipate the reason for his wavering.

"Why don't you tell me what is bothering you," she said, though the patience in her voice now seemed strained.

"Nothing," Henry answered defensively. "I'll see that it's done."

He stood up and walked from the desk, but he paused. She was reminding him to be confident, and she had given into his blackmail almost immediately, and happily so.

He turned back to her.

"I'll speak to Jenny, and I'll take her out for a drink tonight. However, I'll come to your room when I'm done with her, and I want you ready for me in every sense. I want you waiting for me, I want you laying on your bed until the minute I arrive. I also want you in lingerie. But most of all, I want you ready to take my cock. The size will be no surprise to you at this point, so I want your body ready. This time, I want more than your mouth."

Her lips parted a little, apparently taken aback by Henry's forceful command, but, only a few seconds later, she broke into a grin.

"You've got a lot of wants. Don't worry. I'll be ready."

HENRY COULDN'T HELP but feel nervous, and more than a little ridiculous, as he reapproached the reception desk, behind which Jenny was sitting. There was no one in the lobby; even Michael had apparently stepped away from the bar.

Jenny was scrolling on her phone, with one leg crossed over the other. The pleat at her hip seemed almost childish. Henry stared for a moment at the bare skin of her thigh, before remembering his purpose and clearing his throat.

Jenny looked up.

"You were talking to Maria?" she asked, before continuing. "I haven't seen Alan at all today. Did she say anything about him?"

Henry shook his head. "I didn't ask, though."

Jenny looked at him for a few more seconds before her eyes returned to her phone screen.

"Jenny," Henry said.

She looked back up. "Uh-huh?"

"Would you like to get a drink with me, when we're done here?" he asked.

Her eyes widened, and her mouth fell open a degree. She uncrossed her legs, and looked as though she might stand. Instead, she settled back uneasily in her chair and recrossed her legs.

"You mean like a date?" she asked.

"Yes, Jenny, like a date."

She cast an almost panicked glance at the empty barstools across the lobby, as though weighing her options for suitors in right in front of Henry. Perhaps Henry's only saving grace was the fact that he was present, while his rival was not.

"Sure," Jenny said. "We can grab a drink tonight. Where do you want to go?"

Henry didn't even need to think. It was a place that had brought him unimaginable luck, opening doors he had never known existed.

"How about the bar across the street?"

"Alan might see us there," Jenny said. "I think it's one of his favorites."

Henry shook his head. "I don't think he's around today, and I wouldn't care if he saw us there anyway."

"Alright," Jenny said with a shrug. "I guess it's a date."

Chapter Thirteen

Maria lounged behind her husband's desk, though she supposed it was really her desk now. She pushed a handful of papers around using the tip of a pen, ignoring the ink marks that streaked across the polished wooden surface in their wake.

She was bored. The alcohol was gradually deadening in her system, and she felt a little nauseated. Still, cutting her recreation short had been worth it. She cringed internally when she thought of how that hotel guest had droned on, vaguely and pathetically making pass after pass in every brief moment of silence. Maria had steered the conversation toward the hotel staff. She was hardly surprised to learn that Jenny had been quite attentive to his needs, and Henry not so much.

It seemed that Jenny's attempts to capture Michael's attention had been as clumsy as they were endearing. It was mildly interesting, but it was not until Michael related seeing Henry follow Jenny into the women's bathroom, that Maria began seeing the usefulness of her drinking companion.

It seemed she was not alone in being the object of Henry's desire. Though Maria imagined Jenny to be the somewhat lower hanging fruit in the young man's efforts toward erotic stimulation, it was interesting nonetheless.

Then again, Maria had always been vain.

She laughed to herself as she thought about Henry's demand to have her waiting for his arrival, on the bed, in lingerie. She'd do it and, what's more, she'd be looking forward to seeing exactly what Henry had planned for her. There was something amusing about putting herself completely at the mercy of his fumbling desires.

His size was impressive, and it was obvious that he was well aware of this fact, but it was still unclear what use this length and girth could be put to, when entirely under his control.

Chapter Fourteen

At the end of their shift, Jenny asked Henry to meet her at the bar across the street, instead of walking across together as planned. She wanted to go to her bedroom to freshen up.

Henry agreed, and returned briefly to his own bedroom to retrieve the book. He slipped it into his coat pocket, and pulled the garment tight around him as he stepped out of the hotel into the briskly cold air.

At the bar, Henry sat down at a table facing the door, but stood back up the moment he saw Jenny step through the threshold. She was wrapped in a jacket which made her look twice her size, but he could see that she had applied a fresh layer of makeup.

She smiled hesitantly when she saw him and approached the table. She stood above him for a few seconds, before taking off her jacket, and hanging it on the back of her chair. Henry almost felt like he should help her, but, instead, he only watched awkwardly as the jacket slipped from one side while she was trying to take a seat.

"Thank you for joining me," Henry said. "I've been wanting to take you out for a while."

"Have you?" Jenny asked.

"Of course," Henry said.

Jenny said nothing, but stared down at the drinks menu in front of them. When the waiter came over, she surprised Henry by ordering a dry martini, though he was unsure of what exactly he had expected her to drink.

Henry ordered a whiskey, and soaked in the uncomfortable silence which stretched between them the moment the server was gone.

"I asked Maria about Alan," Jenny said, apparently willing to break the silence.

Henry's eyebrows raised, but he said nothing, inviting her to continue.

"She said she doesn't know where he is, and that she hadn't seen him since yesterday evening," Jenny said.

"And she's not worried?" Henry asked.

Jenny shrugged. "Didn't seem to be."

They lapsed into silence again, and Henry was struck by just how uncomfortable a pair they made. He had nothing left to say, so he decided that, though it might be premature, he would follow Maria's advice.

He reached behind himself, into the pocket of his jacket and retrieved the book. He set it down on the table between them, the pornographically photographed platinum blonde staring up at the pair of them, her eyes as wide as her legs.

"Henry—"

Henry thrust out his palm, desperately seeking to silence whatever complaint was seconds from her lips.

"I know. I can't imagine this makes much sense right now," he said.

Though Maria had told him to bring the book, and to place it with confidence, he did not know what came next. He took a deep breath, and tried to remember exactly what the crudely drawn map on the inside of the book looked like. If he could create a kind of talisman of the book, recognizing that it was this very object which had begun to propel him forward, that somehow the way would be revealed to him.

Yet, he found he was still without a clear sense of himself within this new space.

"Jenny, I don't know what to say. The truth is that I find myself at a loss for words whenever I'm around you, and I have no idea how to fix this. I want you to look at me the way you look at the man at the bar, and to think of me as someone you might see a future with, but I have no idea of how to make those desires even close to a reality," he admitted with a clarity that startled him.

Jenny looked at her hands, where they rested dumbly on the table. The waiter returned and set down their drinks, though the fresh silence that stretched between them remained unbroken.

"Henry—"

She cut herself off, and turned to study of her drink. She pressed the stem of the martini glass lightly between her thumb and middle finger, staring at the tension in the pads of her fingertips.

Henry took a deep swallow from his drink. He knew the courage of the liquor would reach him only when it was too late. Still, the warmth which swelled in his chest, and the thin thread of saliva trickling down his throat, at least provided some distraction from Jenny's resumed silence.

"This was a bad idea," Henry said, giving in to his nagging fears.

The situation was too uncomfortable to bear, and he knew she must be overwhelmed by pity for him. More than that, he knew he deserved every ounce of pity he was offered. It was hardly her fault that he was so pathetic, though he wished he could just go back to blaming her for passing him over time and time again.

"No, it's not that," Jenny said. "I guess I'm just confused. Maybe once or twice I thought you were interested, and then the other day you kissed me. I feel like I'm playing catch up, so please just be patient with me."

It didn't sound like a no.

"You're just so beautiful and sweet. I've never felt worthy," Henry said. "I knew you'd be kind to me; you always have been. I could always trust you not to hurt me, but I was afraid that you might mistake offering me pity for kindness."

At this, Jenny's eyes began to well up with tears, but she quickly brushed them away. She lifted the glass to her lips, delicately gripping the glass stem, and took a drink. It seemed her nerves were as affected as Henry's.

"I am so glad that you finally asked," she said simply, setting the drink back down on the table, but appearing steadier.

"So am I," Henry said.

HENRY HAD ENJOYED TWO drinks with Jenny, and then two more after dropping her off by the elevators. It seemed there was no end to the amount of courage he lacked that evening. He wanted to walk straight to Maria's bedroom, knock on the door, and claim the prize he had been imagining for hours, the prize she seemed strangely eager to give.

Yet, he wanted to know just how closely she was following his instructions. Instead of going directly to her bedroom, he returned first to his own. He found his way once again through the hidden hallways to the one-way mirror, where he quickly extinguished his light, and looked through the piece of glass.

Maria was on the bed. She wore a skimpy garment made of lace and ribbons which wound around her body, dipping into and out of sight as it traversed her curves. She held a book in her hands, and her head dipped lazily to the side as she read, keeping her body gloriously on display even in this solitary moment.

The idea that he would soon be there beside her on the bed, that his fingers would study the fabric before delving into an exploration of her naked form was almost overwhelming. His own body immediately responded to the promise of the pleasure which was to come, and the strength of his erection was almost unbearable.

He knew he could not show up at her door so obviously aroused, not without tipping her off to the fact that he had been spying on her. Or worse, she might think that the hardness of his cock had been provoked by the lingering spell of his date with Jenny.

Either possibility was unacceptable, so he wandered the dark hallways, focused on restoring a tenuous equilibrium to his stirred state. He felt his way down the staircase, and brushed his palms over the splintering walls. The sense of danger within darkness gradually provoked a calm within him.

When he finally reached Maria's door, the bright lights and gaudy hotel decorations had forced thoughts of unfettered sexuality from his mind. Instead, he was faced with the door and the woman behind it.

He knocked once and, after a moment, heard quiet footsteps padding toward the threshold.

When Maria answered, she was wrapped in the same silk robe which Henry had seen her in during his first voyeuristic adventure. He was pleased to see that whatever was to be shared with him was hidden from whomever else might have opened the door.

"Come in," Maria said.

Henry stepped past her, and he breathed deep the scent of her perfume. It was floral and woody, balancing the light and the strong, the delicate and the powerful.

It was the scent of Maria, and Henry could not truly understand how fate had placed in his hands the tools to bend her to his will.

Yet, it had, and he would be a fool to not take full advantage.

"How was your date with Jenny?' Maria asked.

Henry shrugged before sitting down at the foot of the bed. It was strange being in the room which he had observed from afar, to experience just how smooth the bedspread was, and how rich the colors of the room and furnishings were.

"It went well," he said. "She told me she was glad that I'd asked her out."

"I'm sure she was," Maria said, sitting down beside him, and clutching two glasses of brandy, one of which she pressed to his hand.

He took a sip and knew that it must have been a fine brandy, though it was wasted on him.

The black silk robe had begun to slip from Maria's shoulder and Henry grasped the material in his fingertips, before helping it off the rest of the way. He could now see just how intricate the design of the teddy was. There were at least three different types of lace, and the thin strips were stitched to black ribbon and gently wound around her body. It was open in a few places, and it was easy to see that this garment was built for access. More difficult to grasp was the fact that it was now worn for his access to her body. A thrill ran down his spine as he realized that she had selected this piece of clothing, knowing that it would be touched by his hands, that the openings would allow his cock to enter her, and that his eyes would enjoy the way the black lace accentuated her assets.

He rested the drink on his knee with one hand, while the other began its preliminary exploration of her breasts. He cupped one breast and then the other, enjoying the supple weight of the flesh, and the slight coarseness of the lace contrasted with the softness of her skin.

His hand moved to her waist, and his palm traced the curve of her hip. He dipped his fingertips beneath the stitched ribbons, and he couldn't help but notice the way her breathing became a little harder.

Eager to get his glass out of the way, he swallowed down the rest of the brandy. Maria took it from his hands, and set both of their empty glasses down on the table. She returned to the bed, but, this time, she pressed her palm to Henry's chest, coaxing him to lie down. She climbed onto the bed and straddled his waist, her knees sinking into the mattress.

She began to carefully unbutton his shirt, sliding her fingernails beneath the fabric and against his chest as she worked her way in agonizingly slow movements toward the end of the shirt, where it rested just a few inches above his throbbing manhood.

She teased his shirt free, her hard nipples grazing his chest through the tight-fitted lace. Henry found himself slipping into a trance as he submitted to her attentions. Her palms ran up and down his torso, seeming to appreciate the light muscularity of his body, though his physique was something he had made a habit of keeping well-hidden in the day to day.

He liked to imagine that she was pleasantly surprised by the condition of his body, and it was with a strange pang that he realized this was the moment he had been preparing for, the moment when this one woman would see the slight definition of his abs, and the gentle swell of muscle in his chest and arms.

Yet, he hadn't wanted to take such a passive role today. Remembering this, he grasped her wrists and pulled her hands back from his body. At this, she was openly surprised, and sat up a little.

"Is everything alright?" she asked.

Without a word, Henry pulled her to the side and sat up, so that he was over her reclining form. She smiled at the reversal of their positions, and opened her legs a little, inviting him in.

He set his hands against the mattress on either side of her shoulders, and he pressed his groin hard against hers. He could not feel the delicate fabric, nor the softness of her sex through his jeans, but he could see the effect of this new friction on the young widow, as he began to roll his hips against her.

Her hands moved to his shoulders, as she drew him down on top of her. He allowed his weight to rest on her in degrees, and it seemed to draw no complaint. His fingers dug into her flesh, as the raw heat of desire and possession ran through him. He wanted to dominate her completely, in a way no man had before.

Then again, he supposed he already did. He knew her deepest secret, and they were bonded by her husband's murder. He knew he should be careful, that he did not yet understand everything she was capable of, but the thick throbbing between his legs made her murderous nature seem a trivial thing.

He stood back up and undid his belt. He unzipped his pants and freed his large, thick erection. His arousal had become almost unbearably painful, and he knew he could not exist another moment except buried deep inside her.

He spread her legs further, and brought his cock's head to the opening in the lingerie over her already wet sex. He plunged his finger inside her, enjoying the warm, slick, swollen orifice against his fingers, before pressing his cock forward, filling her with a single thrust.

She tried to hide the expression of pain which flitted across her face, but Henry had been watching her too carefully. She had known how large he was, but it seemed she was still not entirely prepared.

Maria was tight around him, and he began to move in slow thrusts, almost playing with her, enjoying the feeling of being in control, while she submitted to providing the ultimate pleasure for his deeply stuck cock.

When her slightly pained expressions gave way to small moans of pleasure, he knew she was ready for more. He drew his cock out slowly, before thrusting it back in, allowing every inch of his member to enjoy the tight depths of her passage.

Finally, he could no longer restrain himself. He leaned down and pressed her lips to his as he began to thrust faster. He could feel the jogging of her ample breasts against his chest, as they bounced with every hard thrust. He reached one hand down and grabbed her right breast. With the other, he held the back of her neck, tilting her face towards his. Her eyes were fixed on his, and her brow was creased. Her lips were slightly parted, and small moans of pleasure escaped.

When Henry finally came, it felt as though the very essence of his body had escaped with his semen. He collapsed on top of her, and he felt their intermingled sweat smeared across his chest.

His cock was still swollen and buried deep within her. He lifted himself a little to kiss her, pressing his lips to hers as he felt his cock relaxing within her.

It was the first time he had felt truly fulfilled.

He pulled himself free, and watched transfixed as a dribble of his semen escaped, trickling across her leg and onto the black and gold bedspread.

Henry laid down on the bed beside Maria, and he reached his arm around her, pulling her close.

Maria rested her cheek against his sweat-soaked chest. She was still breathing a little hard, and her red lipstick had been smudged by the kisses he had placed on her lips. He imagined he must look more than a little disheveled himself.

He kissed her forehead lightly, before drawing her even closer.

"Was it everything you imagined?" Maria asked, though there was an edge to her words.

Henry nodded.

"Was it different than with your husband?" Henry asked.

He could feel her smile against his chest.

"Of course it was different," she said.

"Better?" he asked.

Maria nodded. "It was much better."

"Why did you kill him?" Henry asked.

Maria was silent for a moment before answering.

"The idea of him living became unbearable to me," she said. "Even if I'd left, I would never have been able to stand the idea that somehow, somewhere, he was still breathing, living a life that I had both touched and despised."

"Have you killed before?" Henry asked.

Maria shook her head. "I had never wanted to kill someone before my husband, though now I know that I could easily do it again."

If her words were a threat, Henry was beyond caring. He just wanted to focus on holding this astoundingly beautiful woman in his arms, while the rest of the world moved around them.

Chapter Fifteen

There was no doubt that Henry had not thought this thing through before. He believed he had. He could have sworn that he had imagined his first time with Maria over and over again for the better part of a year. In fact, he had imagined them together in nearly every room of the small hotel.

Now, laying beside Maria in the dark of early morning, Henry knew he had never truly given his mind room to wander. The fantasies which had preoccupied him were brief moments, hidden and illicit. He had never imagined falling asleep beside her, or waking to the sound of her gentle, steady breathing. Though he had smelled her perfume many times, he had never conjured the scent it would create when mingled with his own sweat.

He stared at the mirror on the opposite wall, remembering the place where a small taste had become an insatiable hunger. He then felt his true vulnerability, knowing that someone else could be standing in the place that had been his, watching him with a resentment that would not abate.

He drew the bedspread up, covering Maria's shoulder. She turned a little, and he edged closer. This moment between them seemed like all the others they had shared: tenuous. He tried to force the fragility of their fledgling relationship from his mind, but found that within the darkness, fear was his closest companion.

As the daylight grew, he watched with tenderness as Maria gradually awoke. Her eyes fluttered, and the heel of her hand pressed against her forehead. She turned to him, and her smile softened.

"Did you sleep well?" she asked.

Henry nodded. He did not need to ask her how well she slept, as his voyeurism had extended to a loving observation of the woman as she rested.

"We can't be seen together," Maria said, abruptly shaking Henry from whatever fond thoughts had naturally occupied his mind. "Not this soon after Alan's disappearance."

"Of course," Henry murmured. "Whatever you think is best."

Maria broke into a playful grin. "Now, that's not to say we can't have our fun. Are you still thinking about bringing Jenny into this?"

Henry nodded, though it was with a leaden heart. In truth, Maria was more than enough for him, and the idea of dividing his affections brought him nothing but anxiety.

"I think you should try to sleep with her today," Maria said. "She'll be more receptive to the two of us if she feels you both are on more solid ground."

"Maria, I have to confess that I love only you," Henry said. He grasped her hand in his, trying to force his earnestness upon her.

She pressed a light kiss to his fingers.

"That doesn't mean we can't enjoy something a little more risqué," she said. "Besides, being able to show you my affection in such a grand manner would make me happy. You came into my life at the perfect time, and I can't begin to express just how grateful I am."

"But the only person I want is you," Henry repeated.

"And I only want you too, but I can't wait to hear how everything goes with Jenny today," Maria said, running her palm down Henry's chest.

Henry pressed a kiss to her lips, and his hands began their own exploration. He gripped her shoulder lightly as he turned her towards him, before focusing his attention on her breasts. He kneaded the flesh lightly before squeezing, relishing the little yelp it drew from her lips.

Maria shifted, and pressed Henry to his back. Within seconds, she was sitting astride him. She used her weight to stimulate his stiffening member, moving back and forth on top of him. Henry watched entranced as her breasts bounced slightly with the movement. He reached up to cup her breasts, but she quickly brought his hands back down to his sides, pinning them against the mattress.

By this time, Henry's erection had grown rock hard. With little effort, Maria sat up, handlessly positioned herself on the tip of his cock, and sank down, drawing him inside her inch by inch.

Henry groaned as he felt her warm, wet grip around his aching cock. He wanted so badly to move his hips, to pump his cock into her from beneath, but he stopped himself. It was clear she wanted to take control, and he could do nothing else but submit entirely.

He watched as she began to move, establishing a steady rhythm. His eyes wandered over her body hungrily, trying to absorb every fine detail of the entrancing sight.

Maria leaned forward, still gripping his wrists tight. Her breasts were only inches above his chest, jogging back and forth as her rhythm grew faster.

Henry knew he could not last much longer, and soon he let out a small, shuddering moan, and felt himself spill deep inside her.

She stayed on top of him for another moment, before placing a rough kiss to his lips, and falling to the side, where she tucked her body against his.

"I can't wait to hear how your evening with Jenny goes," she whispered in his ear. "Think of how much fun the three of us could have."

Chapter Sixteen

Henry's day seemed to pass in a daze of inactivity, and all too soon it was time for his shift with Jenny. As far as he could tell, there had been no further inquiry into Alan's disappearance. It seemed the man was genuinely unmissed.

Jenny was standing behind the desk, and her eyes flitted to him, before returning to the ground as he approached. She was blushing, and Henry resented the affection she showed him. Spending this kind of time with Jenny could only serve to complicate his relationship with Maria, and he almost wished that Jenny would reject his advances. He might have done something himself, were he not so worried about disappointing Maria.

"Are you free tonight?" Henry asked, leaning against the opposite side of the reception desk.

"I am," she said.

"What would you think about a private dinner, just you and me? We could take one of the unbooked rooms, and enjoy a bottle of wine and takeout from the French restaurant across the street," Henry said.

Jenny's smile wavered. "You want to just go to one of the rooms?"

"Nothing like that," Henry said, though in spite of himself he could feel his blood rising. "You and I have spent countless hours together, but never alone. I thought that being there, just the two of us, might be a nice change."

Jenny nodded, and the surety of her smile returned. "I guess that makes sense. Is there anything I can bring?"

"Just let me take care of you tonight," Henry said.

Henry wasn't worried about getting a room for the night. It was Maria's idea for Jenny and Henry to meet in an unoccupied room, and she had even suggested holding a room back, on the off chance that a local convention ran late. It was unlikely; Henry had never seen the hotel fully booked since he had begun working there.

Maria was even taking care of the food and wine, arranging for everything to be delivered at approximately the time Jenny and Henry's shift ended.

Michael was already at the hotel bar, and Henry couldn't help but notice the way the guest's eyes would return every so often to the distant figure of Jenny. Henry supposed it must have been a real change for Michael, to have the woman who had visibly obsessed over him suddenly ignore him completely, turning her doe eyes to the man who had been by her side from the beginning.

Despite everything, Henry still felt proud to have taken something so seemingly insignificant from this man: this man who had never shown a real interest in Jenny, but who now seemed so perturbed at being ignored.

By the time their shift ended, the hotel lobby was nearly silent. Michael was still by the bar, though the bartender had long since gone home, and Maria was in the back office. Henry went to the hotel room with sweaty palms, knowing that Jenny would join him there within minutes.

The food was delivered just before Jenny arrived, so Henry had time to make a few small preparations. He put a bouquet of flowers in a tall glass on the table, and opened the wine to give it at least a little time to breathe.

He had forgotten about plates, and it seemed Maria had as well, so he simply arranged the silverware around the food, contained as it was in plastic takeout boxes.

A few knocks came at the door, and Henry rose, his heart racing. He opened the door and Jenny stepped through. She was wearing a new dress, this one red with an embroidered detail stitched in black thread around the hem and neckline.

She looked beautiful, freshly made up, and wearing a dress that highlighted her more diminutive assets. Her breasts appeared rounder and perkier than he had ever seen them, and Henry assumed this was the work of a well-engineered bra. He began to wonder just how much of the figure she presented was artificially created, rather than inborn. Still, he kept his thoughts on pleasing Maria, so he drew Jenny against him, pulling her into a warm, gentle kiss.

When they parted, her eyes flitted to the rather unimpressive display of food and drink Henry had put together. Still, she smiled kindly and took a seat when Henry gestured for them to begin the meal.

Henry poured a generous glassful of wine for both the young woman and himself. He poured just a little more for her, hoping that the alcohol would lubricate inevitable silences of their dinner conversation, sticking points he imagined would be numerous.

"Shall we eat?" he said, spearing a green bean with his fork.

Chapter Seventeen

When the reception desk was abandoned, and Henry and Jenny were fully ensconced in their room, Maria wandered into the lobby. She was clearheaded and tense, aware of every sound around her. She only hoped she was not too late.

Michael was sitting at the empty bar, his head buried in his hands. He looked up as she approached. His eyes were well-pressed and bleary, and a reflexive smile crept across his face as he took in his fresh company.

Maria stepped past him, and wordlessly opened the locked compartment beneath the polished, wooden bar top. She pulled out two glasses and a bottle of gin, before filling both glasses nearly halfway.

"Both for you?" Michael asked.

Still silent, Maria slid the second glass to him.

"Cheers," she said, clinking her glass against his.

"To beautiful women, and the men who never had a chance," Michael said with a wink, before taking a long sip.

"And who might those men be?" Maria asked, leaning against the bar to better display the low cut of her neckline.

Michael made a small choking sound as he took his second sip.

"I guess I was thinking mostly about myself," he said, wiping his mouth with the back of his hand.

"My husband's been gone the last few days," Maria said, frowning delicately into her glass. "I'm getting tired of sleeping alone."

Michael's mouth fell open, and he stared at her.

"I don't think I understand," he began.

"I think you do," Maria interrupted. "Meet me in my room in exactly half-an-hour."

She wrote the number down on a napkin and pressed it into his hand.

She downed the rest of the gin in a single swallow before walking away.

MARIA STARED THROUGH the glass, seeing her little world perfectly framed before her. She had taken so much care in creating that room, in furnishing her little cosmos. She now felt somehow apart from it, seeing her pathetic existence through another's eyes.

She imagined what she must have looked like, laying in the bed, having sex with her late husband, and even tending to herself during moments of solitude, or at least those moments in which she had imagined herself to be alone.

Now, she turned from the glass with a sense of finality, of destiny soon to be fulfilled. She snaked through the dark hallways and old stairs, knowing that she would have company in a matter of minutes.

She had no sooner reentered the bedroom than a knock came at the door. She answered, and Michael stood in the doorway. It was clear that he had continued imbibing after her departure, perhaps trying to summon up the courage to actually meet her. Yet, this felt unlikely. Michael seemed like the kind of man who was no stranger to casual trysts.

Maria began running hot water into the bathtub, before inviting him in. He immediately sat down on the bed, and began unbuttoning his shirt.

"Wait," Maria said. "Why don't we take our time with this."

Michael looked around the room, and his eyebrows raised.

"What did you have in mind?" he asked.

"I know this may sound a little silly," Maria said, "but my husband never indulges me."

"What is it?"

"Would you like to take a bath together? I have the tub filling now, and I brought some oils I think you'll enjoy. I hope a soak and massage before doesn't sound too bad." She made a small pleading motion with her hands. "Please do this with me, and the rest of the evening, I will do whatever you'd like."

At this promise, Michael's eyes widened, and a grin spread across his face.

"Well, since you put it like that," he said.

He followed her into the bathroom. There were no oils, but the bath was by now filled with the hottest water the hotel could offer. Michael put his hands around Maria's waist and she put her arms around his neck. She gently guided him to sit at the edge of the bathtub.

He looked up at her, clearly expecting a kiss. She pressed her fingers to his lips, teasing only a little. She touched the front of his throat lightly, tilting his face towards her.

"I am sorry," she said.

She placed her palm squarely against his chest, before shoving with all her force. This sent the man sprawling backwards into the tub. His head slammed against the tiled wall behind him, but not hard enough to render him unconscious.

He seemed momentarily dazed, but soon scrambled to find a grip on the porcelain tub. He tried to pull himself up, but his soaking wet suit, and slightly inebriated state made his struggle all the more difficult.

Maria pulled a knife from beneath the bathmat, and began to stab wildly. The knife missed more often than it struck, but the heat of the water and the violence of Michael's struggle for survival made his blood flow quickly.

It was only a matter of minutes, minutes spent struggling against the onslaught of stabs and shoves which sent him sprawling back into the bathtub and against the wall, before he was finally still. The water surrounding the suit-clad man was crimson, and his face had dipped beneath the water.

This time, Maria did not need to ensure he was dead with any small tricks. It was clear by the sheer amount of time his face spent beneath the water, that the perennial guest had finally checked out.

Maria spent the remainder of her time wiping down the knife, and cleaning her fingerprints from the door handles. There was only one thing left to do. She retrieved a small plastic bag from her purse and began her preparation of the knife.

Chapter Eighteen

Their meal had ended, and the bottle of wine had been emptied to the final drop. Both Henry and Jenny seemed to deliberately avoid looking in the direction of the king size bed next to them.

Perhaps it was boldness inspired by the two glasses of wine she'd drunk, or perhaps because she realized Henry was not going to make a move, but Jenny suddenly stood up from her chair. She took Henry by the hand and wordlessly led him to the foot of the bed, where they sat down side by side.

"Thank you for dinner," she said.

She wouldn't meet his eyes, but her hand found his. Henry took a deep breath, trying to focus on the task ahead. He thought of the disappointment Maria would suffer should he prove unable, so he fixed his mind on the seduction of Jenny.

He took her jaw in his hand, tilting her face toward his. He pressed a firm kiss to her lips, feeling her mouth open a little. In response, he used his tongue to explore the part of her lips, and was gratified by her response in like.

He slid his other hand over the front of her dress, gently cupping her breast. He could feel the thick layer of padding, and pressed his fingertips a little harder, searching for some hint of living flesh past the artifice Jenny had employed.

Her hand moved to his leg, and gently stroked upward. Her fingertips found the end of his shirt, and slipped beneath, brushing his stomach, and moving upwards to his chest. Henry felt his muscles subconsciously tighten, trying to present his physique well, despite his own ambivalence.

Henry shifted to the side, and laid Jenny down on the bed. Her legs spread, and he slid between them, pressing his hips between her thighs. He began to move gently, the material of his pants and her dress creating friction between them.

Jenny's eyes were locked on his, and Henry's hands moved to her waist, gripping her tight, and holding her fast against his movement. He enjoyed the feel of her beneath him, and felt a thrill run through his body watching her reaction.

So, it came as a surprise even to himself when Henry stood up.

Jenny propped herself up on her elbows and shot Henry a questioning glance. "Is everything alright?" she asked.

Henry nodded, tugging at his shirt collar.

"Everything's fine. I just think I need more time; this is moving too quickly."

"I completely understand," Jenny responded, habitual apology bleeding into her voice.

"Maybe we can have dinner tomorrow," Henry said. "We could go to a restaurant, and then try this again."

Jenny nodded, but her brow was knit in confusion. "Of course. Are you sure everything's okay?"

"Yeah, I just have something on my mind, something I'm having trouble shaking."

"Is it Michael?" Jenny asked. "There was never anything between us. I had a crush on him, but that's all. Besides, it's no secret the way you look at Maria."

"I know," Henry said. "I'm not worried about him. I promise, I'll be better tomorrow."

Jenny nodded, forcing a sympathetic smile. "I look forward to it. I really enjoyed our dinner."

"Me too."

HENRY KNOCKED ON THE door, and waited. He heard the light footsteps approach, followed by a long pause. When the door finally opened, he saw Maria, dressed in a red negligee, and holding a glass of brandy in her hand.

"How did things go with Jenny?" she asked, stepping aside so Henry could enter.

Henry sat down in an armchair, and rubbed his face hard with the heel of his hand.

"I couldn't do it," he admitted. "We had dinner, and kissed for a little while, but I just couldn't have sex with her. It felt like I was being unfaithful."

Maria poured a heavy dose of brandy, which she pressed into Henry's hand, before taking a seat in his lap.

"That's very sweet. And maybe it's not the worst thing in the world, to make her wait. It's more like a proper courtship that way," she said.

Henry took a sip of brandy, and rested his other hand on Maria's hip. This was where he wanted to be: sitting with the woman he loved in his lap, warmed by her feminine charms. He couldn't imagine that there was a man in the world happier than he was in that moment.

Maria pressed her red-painted lips to his, gently and chastely reminding him that his desires were reciprocated, that he was finally seen.

The brandy warmed his chest, and emboldened him. He kissed Maria's neck, and felt her body soften in response to his affection. She set down her drink and wrapped her arms around him, turning so that her legs were on either side of his hips. The red, silken material of her negligee rose, giving Henry a glimpse of the naked body which lay beneath. He was gratified to see that she wasn't wearing any panties, and his palms explored the naked curvature of her ass.

She stood, and led Henry to the vanity: the place where she had been sitting the first time he had ever watched her through the one-way mirror. She had brushed her hair with a look of such sorrowful concentration, as though tending to herself in those small ways was the only source of comfort afforded to someone as despondent as herself.

Yet, those following days had seen her become the woman who stood before Henry now: a woman who had seized a moment: realizing the full extent of her power, and unfettering herself from the aspects of her life which brought reliance on emptiness.

Maria moved aside the chair, and slipped free from the negligee. She placed her hands on the edge of the vanity table, and watched Henry in the mirror as he unzipped his pants, freeing an erection which had been begging for release since the moment she had kissed him.

He pressed the tip against her entrance and drove forward. She gasped, and moved her hips back to make sure that every inch of his rock-hard cock was buried in her body. He began to thrust, enjoying the way her expression became one of pure pleasure, as her body gladly accepted his driving shaft. Her breasts bounced and swayed, and her lips parted in a moan.

Soon, Henry was bucking hard against her and the vanity rattled against the wall. Bottles of perfume and beauty accouterments shifted and fell to the ground as the passion of their lovemaking shook the table. Henry felt ecstasy growing in the pit of his stomach as he watched Maria orgasm, biting back a moan as she steadied herself, gripping the edge of the table even tighter.

Henry's own orgasm followed quickly, and he held her waist tight as he spilled himself deep inside of her, pressing his body impossibly close to hers and trying to stay there, in that moment, for as long as he possibly could. If he could have clung to her any tighter, he would have, but he had to satisfy himself with the knowledge that he had filled this beautiful creature with his essence, that he had possessed her both inside and out.

AFTERWARD, THEY LAY in bed beside one another. Henry wrapped his arms around Maria, holding her tight. He pressed a kiss to her cheek, and the sheen of sweat still covering his body seemed to glue them to one another.

Maria rolled over a little, and propped herself up on one elbow. She tucked her hair behind one ear, and looked down at Henry, gently stroking his cheek.

"I've enjoyed our time together," Maria said. "I can't believe it's coming to an end."

Panic flashed through Henry, and he sat up quickly, pushing her hand from his cheek.

"What do you mean?" he asked.

"I mean that I'll be calling the police soon. I think they'll be very interested in the dead man in your room. A man you seem to have killed," Maria murmured as she ran her fingers down his chest. "Then again, jealousy has always been one of your weaknesses."

"What are you talking about?" Henry asked.

Maria shrugged and rolled onto her back.

Henry seized her by the shoulder. "What are you talking about?" he repeated.

Maria didn't look at him, instead allowing her eyes to wander the ceiling in a studied show of disinterest.

"Go see for yourself."

Chapter Nineteen

Henry dressed quickly and raced to his room, barefoot and with his shirt unbuttoned. The moments between Maria's door and his seemed to pass by with excruciating slowness, yet at the same time in a heady blur.

Deep within, he understood Maria's meaning completely, but he would not let himself believe that she would try to destroy him so completely. As he used his keycard to open the door, he braced himself for what he would find inside. Countless scenarios ran through his head, but nothing could prepare him for what awaited.

The bathroom was covered in water and blood, and Henry's bare feet slid on the slippery mixture which suffocated the tile floor. There was a fully clothed body floating face down in the bath, and a knife rested nearby on the floor.

Henry knew he had to get the body out of the bath, and away from the room before the police could arrive, yet there was no way he could clean up the blood which was splattered on the walls and across the floor. It was simply too much.

So, he narrowed his focus, blindering himself to the reality of the situation which lay before him. He could worry about only one thing. He grabbed the corpse beneath the shoulders and hauled the body from the bath. He slipped and fell, the body landing on top of him, soaking his clothing in the same bloody mixture which filled the bathtub.

Beneath his shoulder rested the knife, and he picked it up and threw it to the side, before grabbing the corpse by the wrist and dragging the deceased man toward the bedroom. He knew he was making countless mistakes, that if he looked at the situation objectively, he would see that he was only making things worse.

However, panic had taken hold of his thinking, and everything was converted to overly simplistic actions. Michael's corpse was in Henry's bathroom, and that needed to be rectified. Henry grabbed the bedspread and laid it on the floor, before rolling the corpse into the covers. It was just like what he had seen Maria do, and he repeated this to himself. He ignored the way the blood was spreading to the carpet, and further soaking his clothing. He forced himself to look away from the crimson fluid which now coated his forearms.

A knock came at the door, but Henry ignored it. He walked to the bathroom and tried to soak up the bloody water with the towels and bathrobe that had been hanging by the door. He opened the drain to the bathtub, and watched as the water began to recede, but far too slowly.

The knocking at the door had turned into pounding, until Henry heard the familiar electronic spasm of the keycard reader, followed by the sound of the mechanical lock turning. He retreated further into the bathroom, trying desperately to find a way to hide himself, but finding no refuge.

FOUR POLICE OFFICER stormed the room, their weapons were drawn and they were wearing bulletproof vests. Two stayed in the bedroom, while the other two entered the bathroom.

"Put your hands up," one of the officers said, training his gun on Henry.

The other officer moved forward with a brutal quickness. He forced Henry to turn, before putting him in handcuffs. Henry could not even find the breath to protest, or offer even a word in his defense. He was blinded by the ruthless, crimson scene surrounding him.

It was then that he saw the knife. It lay against the wall, where he had thrown it earlier. There were a few light-colored strands at the hilt, glued to the blade with fresh blood. They were too light to be either Maria's hair or Michael's.

Henry had only to think for a moment before he realized whose hair it was. Alan's.

MARIA SAT BEHIND THE reception desk and watched as Henry was led out by the police officers. A crime scene crew had already entered the building. Maria had insisted that they use the back entrance, to avoid stirring up concern among their guests. Of course, with Michael dead, the lobby was empty apart from herself and Jenny.

Henry tried to say something, but the police officers propelled him forward.

Maria watched with a kind of numb amusement as Henry was shoved through the door and out onto the sidewalk, where he was quickly placed in a waiting police car.

Chapter Twenty

Over the following months, there was not a single day that Jenny's eyes were not red from late nights spent crying. She blamed herself for Michael's death, believing that she had somehow encouraged Henry to take the life of the man she had shown interest in.

Maria didn't try too hard to console her.

During the trial, Henry seemed more interested in exchanging glances with Maria than he did in proving his innocence. Maria found herself wearing increasingly provocative clothing to court, no longer feeling it necessary to portray herself as the grieving widow.

The more time she spent in the courthouse, wordlessly drinking in Henry's needy energy, the more she understood that he was not fighting for himself, but rather for her. It seemed he had not shared crucial information with his defense, as she never again saw the photos he had taken the night she killed her husband.

Instead, he maintained his innocence, while offering nothing to back his claim. Maria was almost touched by the gesture, and felt a kind of sadness when the jury quickly handed down a guilty verdict and Henry's head bowed low as he heard their decision.

Maria could only imagine the despair he must have felt, but she focused instead on the protection he had afforded her. She had an idea of how exactly to make it up to him, and the prospect filled her with a kind of amusement. In fact, she nearly laughed aloud in the middle of the courtroom.

She offered Henry her most winning smile as he was escorted from the room. He must have thought she was mocking him, lording her victory during his darkest hour. Yet, when he realized just what her plan was, he would hardly begrudge her a smile.

Yes, she would make it up to him in spectacular fashion, and he would thank her for it. Though she'd taken his life from him, he would thank her for it.

Chapter Twenty-One

When the guard showed Maria into the room, Henry was already seated at one of the metal tables. He was dressed in an orange jumpsuit, which was rolled up at the sleeves affording his visitor a view of his lean, toned forearms. He looked up when she entered, and his eyes widened.

Henry stood up.

"They told me I had a visitor, but I had no idea..." he trailed off.

Maria said nothing, she just walked to the chair opposite his and sat down. After a moment of hesitation, he followed her lead.

"What are you doing here?" he asked.

She leaned back and smiled. "Can't you guess?"

He frowned, but seemed to consider her in all seriousness.

"I saw you every day of the trial," he said, his words were measured. "I'm sure you know I didn't give any of the photos to my lawyer. Is that why you came?"

"In a sense," she answered.

"You want to make sure I've gotten rid of them," Henry said, slumping down in his chair. If he had ever thought there was another reason for her visit, that remnant of hope was destroyed before her eyes.

Maria shrugged. "I don't care if you kept them or not. I'm sure you know that the knife in the photos and the knife they recovered are not the same. The fact that my husband's hair was practically glued to the hilt with blood would make searching for a second weapon, one that truly was never used to stab anyone, almost ridiculous."

Henry's fingers had found the side of the table, and they twisted around the cold edge.

"So, why are you here?" he asked again, though there was a weakness to his voice, as though he was no longer expecting a real answer.

"I'm here for you," she said.

Henry's eyes fixed on her hands, as she brought them to the table's cold, reflective surface. A gold wedding band rested on her thumb, and she slipped it off. She slid it across the table, until her fingertips brushed Henry's.

"I don't know if they'll let you keep it," she said.

Henry stared down at the ring, before picking it up. He turned it over in his fingers, until the small loop of metal came to rest on his left ring finger. It slid down one knuckle, resting awkwardly.

"You want to marry me?" he asked.

"You'll be eligible for parole in twenty years. Maybe it only seems like a long time," she answered.

Henry pressed the ring down a little, until it came to a tight resting place on his finger.

"I accept."

Epilogue

Henry stared at the red mark on his calendar: the only notation on an otherwise blank grid. Maria would be visiting him soon. When they had married in a small prison chapel affair, he had been convinced that this was all some joke that only Maria understood. He had assumed she would never see him again, but he had been very much mistaken.

Maria visited regularly for conjugal visits. During these brief encounters, she would give herself to him completely, but only for a moment. Just as he was reaching the heights of ecstasy, she would remove a small pin she had hidden somewhere in her clothing, and prick the pad of each finger on her right hand.

She would caress his body with her bloody fingertips, bringing stripes of tortured flesh to the surface, scarring his skin just as he reached the pinnacle of their sexual union. In his mind, pain and pleasure had become inextricably linked.

Yet, he had never refused to see her. No matter what she did to him, he would accept it wholeheartedly. Possessing her in some way was the only shred of pride he nursed in the hellhole of his confinement. To know that she belonged to him was his sole comfort, and he would not relinquish this for anything.

Perhaps he had begun to see her as Alan had those years before, as nothing more than something to own: a belonging to have for the sake of having.

In the dark of night, these thoughts would cross Henry's mind. He would wonder at the price he had paid, but then he would think of Maria.

Also by Lydia Harbinger

The Man in the Wall
Fallen Under
The Blood of Maria

Watch for more at https://www.lydiaharbinger.com/.

www.ingramcontent.com/pod-product-compliance
Lightning Source LLC
Chambersburg PA
CBHW031451130726
47989CB00003B/1344